BEATNIK RUTABAGAS FROM BEYOND THE STARS

QUENTIN DODD

BEATNIK RUTABAGAS FROM BEYOND THE STARS

FARRAR STRAUS GIROUX NEW YORK

Copyright © 2001 by Quentin Dodd
Distributed in Canada by Douglas & McIntyre Ltd.
Printed in the United States of America
Designed by Judith M. Lanfredi
First edition, 2001
10 9 8 7 6 5 4 3 2 1

Library of Congress Cataloging-in-Publication Data
Dodd, Quentin, 1972–
    Beatnik rutabagas from beyond the stars / Quentin Dodd.— 1st ed.
       p. cm.
    Summary: Whisked away on space ships to serve as generals of opposing armies, best
friends and sci-fi movie fans Walter Nutria and Yselle Meridian soon convince the
aliens they must work together against the real menaces, Space Mice from Galaxy
Four and their leader, The Boss.
    ISBN 0-374-30515-3
    [1. Outer space—Fiction.   2. Science fiction.   3. Humorous stories.]   I. Title.

PZ7.D66273 Be 2001
[Fic]—dc21
                                                                00-140217

For Paula

BEATNIK RUTABAGAS FROM BEYOND THE STARS

1

It was a beautiful Tuesday afternoon in early April. Song-birds were chirping, deep green leaves were appearing on the trees of East Weston, and Walter Nutria was sitting on the couch in Yselle Meridian's rec room, watching *Invasion of the Saucer Men*.

Walter and Yselle had been friends ever since a Halloween party in the fifth grade, when they had both dressed as Gort, the robot from *The Day the Earth Stood Still*. By the time they were freshmen in high school, they had watched hundreds of movies together. Mostly at Yselle's house. Walter's mother didn't approve of Yselle. She hadn't liked Yselle four years ago, when Yselle first visited Walter's house carrying a copy of *20 Million Miles to Earth* in her Godzilla backpack. Mrs. Nutria liked Yselle even less now with a punk haircut and tapes of *Devil Girl from Mars* and *Plan 9 from Outer Space*. Walter had never been able to figure out why.

On the screen, Gloria Castillo was in hysterics as the saucer men ran around in the underbrush.

"Her makeup is different than it was in *Teenage Monster*," Yselle said. "Do you think she looks better here?"

Walter shrugged. "Yeah, probably."

"Better than Lorna in *Monster from Green Hell*?"

"Very funny." A while ago Walter had told Yselle how much he'd liked that movie, not because of the radioactive giant wasps but because of the actress Barbara Turner. Yselle still kidded him about it, and Walter never failed to get embarrassed. Walter pushed himself down into the couch cushions and watched the rest of the movie without looking at Yselle.

By the time the saucer men had been defeated, Yselle's dad was ready to drive her to her piano lesson, so Walter had to go home.

They waited on the porch as Yselle's dad pulled the car around. "Will I see you in school tomorrow?" she asked.

"Probably not." Although Walter was only a freshman at East Weston Northside High, he was already an expert at skipping class. His last two periods of the day were gym and choir, and he had learned quickly how to get out of both of them. Coach Flowers, the gym teacher, didn't believe in taking attendance. His classes were always half empty, but the coach never seemed to notice. In choir, the class was much too big for Miss Wizneuski to know everyone by sight, so as long as someone said "present" when Walter's name was called, he was safe. Walter had made a deal with Timmy Arbogast to take care of this. Walter would answer "present" for Timmy in study hall, and Timmy would answer for Walter in choir. That way, Timmy Arbogast got to take a mid-morning nap, and Walter's afternoons were pretty much his to do with as he liked. He always hoped Yselle would duck out early with him, but it never happened. Her last class of the day was Latin, where the teacher was conscientious about accurate roll calls.

Tomorrow, Walter was especially eager to leave as soon as possible. *The Eye Creatures* and *Zontar, the Thing from Venus* were arriving at Honest Bob's Video Palace, and he wanted to make sure he got them before anyone else.

Yselle got in the car. Walter waved goodbye and started walking. It was still early, and Walter didn't feel like going home yet. Instead, he set off toward the center of town, which took him past the East Weston Northside High building.

Seeing the school started Walter thinking. In a lot of ways, the classes he skipped were easier to tolerate than the ones he stayed for. He began each day with Mrs. Baucomb, who taught history by reading straight from the textbook in a flat, drawn-out voice that never changed: "In . . . nineteen . . . twenty . . . Warren . . . G. . . . Harding . . . was . . . elected . . ."

After that was English, then economics. They weren't bad by themselves, but by the time Walter got there, his brain was so numb from sitting through history that he could never get himself to pay attention. Then he had study hall, and after that was the class he really hated: freshman biology with Mr. Murphy.

Mr. Murphy loved skinks. He had hundreds of the small, unhappy-looking lizards living in glass terrariums, and he often left the class sitting in silence while he checked on each one, making sure the skinks were content. Early in the year,

Walter had learned that if you wanted a good grade in freshman biology, all your projects and reports had to have something to do with skinks. A good paper about penguins would get a C or a D, while a bad paper about ferns, if it happened to mention the North American web-footed skink, would get an A. At first this was annoying, since Mr. Murphy never seemed to care if the projects were any good or not. The only thing that mattered was whether they contained the magic word *skink*. Once Walter had realized what was going on, it became like a kind of game, trying to fit information about skinks into projects on every conceivable subject. But the fun had faded fast. In his own way, Mr. Murphy and his skink mania was as bad as Mrs. Baucomb.

Now Walter copied his reports straight out of the encyclopedia, with random sentences about skinks tossed in, and tried to stay awake in class. He hadn't gotten a bad grade in biology for months.

Stopping to tie his shoe, Walter thought about where to go now. His uncle, Horton Nutria, owned a pool hall in East Weston, but Walter didn't go there very often. Walter's parents (especially his dad, who was Horton's brother) didn't approve of Horton Nutria or the people who spent time in the pool hall, and they had ordered Walter to stay away. His parents were bent on keeping Walter away from "bad influences" and were always forbidding him to do things or see people. Last year Walter's mother had read a newspaper article about a group of kids in Brockenborough who had put some dead bugs in candy wrappers and sold them to other kids as real candy. From then on, Walter's mother had refused to let him buy candy of any kind, even from the store, saying, "You never know, Walter, there *could* be something terrible in there. *You never know.*"

Walter thought this was unreasonable, but he had stopped trying to talk to his parents about it. Just like in school, he had learned that it was easier to give up than it was to try to change anything. Mr. Murphy would never hand out a good grade to a report with no skinks, and his parents would never let him spend time at his uncle's pool hall. It didn't make sense, but Walter couldn't do anything about it.

2

Since the pool hall was off-limits, Walter decided to visit
The Lonesome Skillet Café, a run-down diner in downtown
East Weston. He could spend an hour in there, and then it
would be time to head home for supper. Walter often spent
his afternoons at The Lonesome Skillet. Joe, the owner, always asked why he wasn't in school, but as long as Walter
could come up with a creative excuse, Joe would let him stay.

Yesterday he had told Joe that an anaconda from one of the
biology classrooms had gotten loose and eaten three teachers
before the school was evacuated. It was pretty lame, but it
had been good enough for Joe to let him stay there all afternoon, drinking Joe's experimental milk shakes and playing the
antique arcade games that stood along the back wall.

Walter's favorite was the mechanical baseball game. Its
coin mechanism was broken, so he was able to play as long as
he wanted on one nickel. Walter suspected that Joe would fix
it if he knew, so he always pretended to add more coins whenever Joe was looking.

As Walter walked downhill toward the courthouse and the Masonic temple, the sky suddenly got darker, as if a fast-moving cloud had covered up the sun.

But there wasn't any sun. It had been overcast all day.

What was going on? Walter turned around and looked up. There it was. Hovering just above the treetops was a flying saucer. It was as big as a house, shaped like a stainless-steel Frisbee with a big bulge in the middle. It spun rapidly, giving off a high whining sound that Walter could just barely hear.

As he stared up at it, a port opened on the underside. A greenish light spilled out, and something began to emerge from the opening.

It was a segmented metal tube that writhed and twisted as it snaked its way down from the spaceship. On the end of the tube was a brown lumpy thing. As it got closer to the ground, Walter saw that it was a giant baseball glove.

Walter stood rooted to the spot, bathed in the greenish light, as the tube and glove descended toward him and gently settled to the ground. The glove smelled like onion soup and old leather. Pinned in the middle was a note, written on yellow legal paper.

It read: "Our gripper device is broken. Please climb on. Thank you."

This was without a doubt the strangest thing that had ever happened to Walter Nutria in his entire life. As he stared at the giant baseball glove, he was surprised to realize that he wasn't acting like people usually did in the movies. He wasn't panicking. He wasn't running around screaming. He wasn't wondering Why me? or What's happening? Instead, he found himself thinking, It's about time. Walter had been walking through boring day after boring day here in East Weston, and now, finally, something interesting had arrived.

He took a quick look up and down Mordant Boulevard to make sure no one was watching (no one was) and jumped aboard the alien baseball glove.

With a jerk like an old roller coaster getting into gear, the glove rose up again, carrying him toward the spaceship and the strange light. The closer Walter got, the brighter the light grew, until he had to cover his eyes against it.

The glove and its passenger disappeared into the flying saucer, and the port closed behind them. A few seconds later, with no more noise than the high whine, the spacecraft zoomed over East Weston and disappeared into the stratosphere.

When he uncovered his eyes, Walter saw that he was standing in the middle of a darkened, circular room. Tiny colored lights were flashing on strange instruments, and he could barely make out shadowy figures in the gloom.

"Welcome," said a voice. "We apologize for the indignity of your arrival, but the grip actuator on our retrieval glove was stolen by Space Mice from Galaxy Four. Would you care for some tea?"

Walter squinted into the darkness, trying to make out who was speaking. "What kind do you have?"

"We have Darjeeling and Prince of Wales. There are also muffins. We stopped at a Safeway before picking you up."

"I'll take Prince of Wales. With sugar. And a muffin." Walter had skipped lunch that day, planning to blow his lunch money later at The Lonesome Skillet Café.

Two of the dark shapes huddled together, and Walter heard bits of a whispered conversation. Finally, the voice spoke again: "We have banana-nut muffins and raisin muffins. Please choose one. We do not have whole-wheat. We apologize."

"That's okay. I'll take banana. And why is it so dark in here?"

"Please forgive us, Walter Nutria," the voice said. "We need your assistance desperately, but we are afraid that our appearance will be frightening to you. Therefore, we planned to keep the interior dark, so as not to be traumatizing."

"And then you would turn up the lights later, once I'd gotten used to you?" Walter asked.

"What?" The voice sounded confused.

"When were you going to turn up the lights?"

"We . . . weren't."

"So you can see in the dark like this?"

There was a pause. "No."

"Maybe you'd better turn on the lights," Walter suggested.

"But you may be horrified, and we cannot afford to have you turn against us."

"It'll be all right, I promise."

"If you think it's best." The voice sighed. "But remember, Walter Nutria, we find your appearance three times as hideous as you may find ours."

"Thank you," said Walter.

The lights came on and he saw his alien associates for the first time.

Walter stumbled backward. He had been expecting the worst, something purple and slimy with bloodshot bug eyes and a segmented exoskeleton. He had been expecting fangs dripping with venom and deadly ray-blaster pistols.

He had not been expecting this.

The aliens all looked like chubby middle-aged men. They wore identical red outfits that looked like too-tight pajamas with built-in feet, mittens, and hoods. Their noses were big and lumpy, and they all needed a shave.

In short, the aliens, every one of them, looked exactly like his uncle, Horton Nutria.

One of them took a step toward him, holding out a large mug and a plate with a muffin on it.

"Your tea is ready," it said.

3

"You guys look just like—"

The alien held up a red-mittened hand. "Don't say it. You have a cousin who looks just like us. Or your postman could be our identical twin. Or you have an aunt on Planet Vorag-7 who is the spitting image of us."

"We've heard it all before," said another alien.

"It's our curse," said a third.

"But who are you?" Walter asked, taking the tea and muffin.

"Excuse our bad manners," said the first alien. "Allow me to introduce myself. I am Uxno, captain of this ship. It is the *Gilded Excelsior*, flagship of the Planet Lirg battle fleet and the pride of our Flying Saucer Corps." Uxno pointed to the second alien. "This is Snartmer, my associate captain." The third alien was introduced as "my sister, Chief Engineer Voo."

Voo looked exactly like Uxno and Snartmer, who looked exactly like Walter's uncle, Horton Nutria. Walter raised an eyebrow. "Sister?"

"Wanna make something of it?" Voo demanded, folding her arms.

"Voo! That is no way to address an honored guest. Bad engineer!" Captain Uxno scowled at Voo. "Go check the Maintenance Deck. If you saw one Space Mouse from Galaxy Four, there are probably more."

Grumbling, Voo waddled off and disappeared down a flight of stairs.

"Please forgive us, Walter Nutria," Uxno said. "Voo is young and stupid. She does not realize the gravity of the situation and your absolutely vital importance to the Lirgonian people."

Walter took a sip of the tea. It was very good.

"You see, our tea-brewing technology is light-years ahead of yours," said Snartmer.

"I believe it."

"The muffins might be a little dry. They were on sale."

"That's all right." Walter bit into the muffin. "You said I was so important to you. Why? What's going on?"

Uxno nodded. "Perhaps you're right, Walter Nutria—"

"Just Walter, please."

"As you wish. You have had tea and a muffin. Perhaps it is best to address the important matter now. You can meet the rest of the crew later," he said, indicating the dozens of Lirgonians who were operating control consoles all around the interior of the saucer, pretending not to listen in. "Please have a seat."

A comfortable chair of ultramodern design, upholstered in white vinyl, rose from the floor next to Walter. Walter sat down, and Uxno began to lecture.

"For centuries on end," Uxno said, "we Lirgonians have

been at war with the dreaded Wotwots. The Wotwots are a savage culture, bent on total subjugation of the universe, or at the very least subjugation of that part of the universe that contains Lirgonians."

"Either way, that's pretty bad for us," added Snartmer.

"Exactly. The Wotwots are petty and cruel, and have no sense of aesthetics. They are widely regarded as being the worst prom dates in the universe. But that does not prevent them from being crafty warriors, and in our long history of conflict, neither side has been able to grasp the upper hand, shake it firmly, and seize the golden apples of victory."

"Until now," Snartmer added.

"Until, as he says, now."

Walter looked from Uxno to Snartmer and back again. "What do you mean?"

"We have you!"

"You!" Snartmer echoed.

"Me?"

"Walter Nutria—of Earth!"

"Earth!"

"Earth?"

Uxno started pacing in small circles around Walter's chair. "You see, the Lirgonian Executive Committee—"

"Which is to say, Captain Uxno, myself, and the president of Planet Lirg," added Snartmer.

"The Lirgonian Executive Committee has decided that what we need in the war against the Wotwots is a general."

"Actually, we were talking to Mong Overthruster at the Spaceline Cafeteria, and he was the one who came up with the idea," added Snartmer.

"That's beside the point. We needed a leader, a brilliant strategist, someone resourceful and cunning who could lead our battle fleet to swift victory!"

"And we couldn't find anyone like that on Lirg," added Snartmer.

"That's correct. So the crew of the *Gilded Excelsior* undertook a survey of all the civilizations in the cosmos, evaluating each one to determine their skill at formulating battle tactics. That led us, naturally, to Planet Earth."

"Mong Overthruster suggested we start there," added Snartmer.

"Once on Earth, we studied your society, walking freely through your video rental stores and discount theaters. There we made a surprising discovery."

"You guys have done this before," interjected Snartmer.

"Exactly! Nearly half of your motion-picture entertainment was about courageous Earth people fighting off alien invaders, often against incredible odds! Soon it became clear to us that every single inhabitant of Planet Earth must be an expert in space conflicts! It was the perfect opportunity!"

"So we checked the video rental records to find out who had seen the most films. That person would obviously be the greatest general," added Snartmer.

Uxno stopped pacing and stood directly in front of Walter. "We hope you can fathom how great an honor we have bestowed upon you, Walter Nutria. The entire Lirgonian people are counting on your bravery and skill. Will you be our general?"

"Look, I think you've made a mistake—"

"This is no time for false modesty!" Captain Uxno pleaded. "Will you help us?"

Walter hesitated for a minute, as beads of sweat ran down Uxno's and Snartmer's dimply cheeks.

Now that he thought about it, he *had* seen a lot of science-fiction movies. Maybe the Lirgonians had a point. And anyway, what else did he have to do? If he told the aliens no, all he had to look forward to on Earth was The Lonesome Skillet Café. There was always his uncle Horton Nutria's pool hall, Walter supposed, but that would enrage his parents if they ever found out. And the pool hall didn't even have a TV. None of those options sounded very exciting.

"All right," Walter said finally. "I'll do it."

4

A cry of joy went up from every red-pajamaed Lirgonian aboard the *Gilded Excelsior*.

"We really ought to go back to Earth for a minute," Walter said. "I need to tell my mom where I'm going."

Uxno beamed at him. "No need. The Automatic Trans-Spatial Excuse Generator has taken care of that for you." He spun around and pointed to a row of video screens. "Activate the Long-Distance Viewing Apparatus!"

The largest screen flashed up a wall of static, which slowly dissolved to reveal the kitchen of the Nutria house. As Walter watched, the image zoomed in on the kitchen table, showing a note written on yellow legal paper. It read:

Dear Mother—I went to the shoe store to buy a cat and some jelly. I will be back in twelve to fifteen years. Love, Walter

Walter leaped up from his chair. "Twelve to fifteen years!"

"That's the long estimate," Snartmer assured him. "We

didn't want your mother to worry. If all goes well and we win the war, we'll all get bonuses. Then we can afford to buy a used time machine, and you'll be home before dinner. Doesn't that sound fair?"

"I don't know. You should have said something about twelve to fifteen years before now."

"But that's not all," Uxno said hurriedly. "In addition to the time machine and the eternal gratitude of Planet Lirg, we have also been authorized to offer you . . ." He paused for effect. "One year's worth of production from Lirg's most prosperous industry!"

An awed hush fell throughout the Lirgonian flying saucer.

"You don't mean . . ." Snartmer gasped.

"I do. The nougat mines!"

Snartmer and Uxno stared at Walter expectantly.

Walter was not sure how he was supposed to react. "Nougat? Like the stuff in candy bars? That kind of nougat?"

"Well, yes," Uxno said. "On your primitive planet all you know how to do with nougat is eat it. But for us, it is much, much more. Nougat is one of the most valuable and versatile substances in the cosmos. It is a source of energy, it is a building material, it fills our swimming pools, and we inflate our beach chairs with it."

Snartmer patted one of the engineering consoles. "The *Gilded Excelsior* even runs on the new Channeling Nougat Interference Space Drive."

"Nougat is the economic backbone of the Seven Orange Galaxies. In fact, this flying saucer you are riding in was built with nougat money.

"So please, Walter Nutria, understand the magnitude of this reward, and the large amount of gratitude with which it is offered," said Uxno.

A clumping noise coming up the stairs announced that Voo had returned to the bridge. "I checked both storage compartments, and I couldn't find any trace of them," she reported.

Uxno frowned. "Once we get to Stoyanovich Station, hire an anti–Space Mouse robot and see if it can sniff them out."

"They may have disappeared, Captain. Sometimes they do."

"That's just a myth, Voo. Space Mice from Galaxy Four can't disappear. They're as normal as you and I."

"But, Uxno . . ."

While Uxno and Voo argued, Snartmer told Walter the story of the Space Mice.

"Space Mice from Galaxy Four are the plague of modern-day intergalactic travel," Snartmer said. "Nobody knows where they came from exactly, except that they were first reported aboard short-distance furniture-hauling ships in Galaxy Four. They hide in the hidden places on a spaceship, like between decks and inside the walls, and they take things."

"Like what?"

"All sorts of things. Engine parts, computer chips, the crews' lunches, anything that's not nailed down. Nobody ever finds the things they take, either. That's where the legend about them being able to disappear comes from. But Uxno's right. It's just a myth. Personally, I think nobody ever finds the stolen stuff because the Space Mice eat it all. But some people say they're just good at hiding things."

"Why don't you set out some traps? They're just mice, right?"

"Believe me, we've tried that. But whenever anyone sets out a trap, the trap disappears."

"You're kidding."

Snartmer shook his head. "Cross my liver and hope to expire. This is the absolute truth. There's even a story, told on the deep-space flying-saucer routes, about a first mate who was determined to catch a Space Mouse from Galaxy Four, and *he* disappeared."

"Now you're kidding."

"Again, I deny that. The best way to deal with them is to get an anti–Space Mouse robot to find the nest, then get rid of whatever they're nesting in."

"And that works?"

"For a little while."

At that moment a voice came over the loudspeaker. "Attention, crew. Attention, crew. The *Gilded Excelsior* is beginning its approach to Space Station Stoyanovich. All crew members to their stations, and make sure that all trauma harnesses are securely fastened. We don't want a repeat of last time. Thank you."

"I'd better go," Snartmer said. "I'm in charge of the auxiliary landing gear." He pointed to the white vinyl chair that still stood in the middle of the floor. "Sit there. You can watch the landing on the big screen."

"What about the trauma harnesses?" Walter shouted to the running red-suited figure. "Do I need one?"

"Probably not. We're pretty good at this anymore."

5

Walter tried to put the thought of his nonexistent trauma harness out of his mind and concentrate on watching the landing.

It wasn't easy.

On the screen he could see the tiny metallic blob that was Space Station Stoyanovich grow larger by the moment. The donut-shaped station spun end-over-end like a coin flipped in the air. As it got closer, the crew of the *Gilded Excelsior* tried to line up their flying saucer with one of the docking ports on the outside of the station. Invariably they would go too far to the left, or up instead of down, and the flying saucer would have to lurch back in the other direction in order to stay on target.

Walter gripped the edge of his chair and tried to resign himself to the idea of crashing.

They sped closer and closer, with Uxno barking orders that the crew rarely seemed to pay attention to. At the last second, with nothing in front of them but the dark metal wall, Uxno shouted, "Stop here!"

There was a sickening halt, then a large docking port filled the viewscreen. The *Gilded Excelsior* drifted inside, coming to rest with a series of muffled clunks and grinds.

The crew broke out in spontaneous applause.

"Stop that!" Uxno shouted. "We have made successful landings several times now, and it is unprofessional to celebrate each one." He turned to Walter. "Especially now that our general is onboard. It makes the wrong impression.

"Anyway," he continued, unbuckling his trauma harness and climbing out of the captain's chair, "we have docked and we are all still uninjured. All of you with duties to perform while we are on Space Station Stoyanovich, go and perform them. All others, amuse yourselves. Walter Nutria and I have important business to conduct."

General chaos followed as each Lirgonian tried to be the first to reach the exit hatch. Uxno dragged Walter through the crowd, shouting, "Make way! Important business!" It helped a little.

Once outside Walter could see that their flying saucer was docked in a bay about the size of a football field. Tube-shaped metal corridors led off in all directions. Some were even in the ceiling and could be reached only by ladders. The crew disappeared quickly, and Uxno started off so fast that Walter had to jog to keep up with him.

Uxno talked as they hurried along. "The owner of this station happens to be an old friend of mine. When she started out, all this was just a repair depot and used-parts warehouse. In fact, some unkind visitors even called it a junkyard. But she's been able to expand since then, and now Space Station Stoyanovich is the most popular general-purpose stop in the whole hemiquadrant."

They crossed an odd-angled intersection of several corridors. Without stopping, Uxno pointed. "Look, there's the Spaceline Cafeteria. The last *Deep Space Freight Hauler* magazine gave it three stars."

Passing by, Walter caught a glimpse of several people hanging around outside. He knew they must be aliens, but they didn't look anything like what he had imagined or seen in the movies. There were some that looked like boxes and some that looked like cooked pasta. Others looked like giant stuffed animals or palm trees with legs. Walter saw a Lirgonian (possibly Snartmer) entering the cafeteria. Compared with everyone else, the Lirgonian was starting to look quite normal. Walter wondered what Uxno's friend Stoyanovich would be like.

There was a banging noise coming from somewhere up ahead, and it got louder the farther they walked. Uxno made a quick right turn into a side passage, and they were at once in another large chamber, bigger than the *Gilded Excelsior*'s docking bay.

"Here we are," Uxno announced.

This was where the noise had been coming from. Two of the palm-tree aliens had a small spaceship on hydraulic lifts and were beating on its underside with mallets. Other space vehicles, all in states of disrepair, were propped up on the floor or hung from the ceiling. Racks of exotic-looking parts stood along the walls, stretching back as far as Walter could see.

"Hey!" Uxno waved at a figure in the distance. "We're here!"

The figure glided toward them rapidly.

"Walter Nutria, I would like to introduce my good friend—who is not only the owner of this space station but a former Miss Congeniality in the Intergalactic Tournament of Beauty—Spherical Mattress Stoyanovich."

Spherical Mattress Stoyanovich was a giant thumb.

The thumb, which stood on its base, was a little bit taller than Uxno and a lot taller than Walter. It slid along the metal floor like a snail.

"Spherical, this is Walter Nutria, our newly appointed general. Walter Nutria is going to lead us to victory against the tasteless Wotwots."

"Nice to meet you, Walter."

Walter didn't see a mouth, or eyes, or a nose, or anything besides the giant thumb itself, but it was talking. And it was talking to him.

"It's nice to meet you, too," Walter replied. His parents had always taught him to be polite, and if there was ever a time when that came in handy, it was now.

"So, you're Uxno's new general. Looks like he made a good choice. I can see the killer instinct in your eyes. The Lirgonians are in good hands."

"Um . . . Thank you."

"Enough idle chitchat!" Uxno drew himself up. "We are here to outfit the flagship for our campaign against the Wotwots. What have you got for us, Spherical?"

"You're lucky," Spherical Mattress Stoyanovich said. "I've had a couple of really nice pieces come in recently. State-of-the-art in serious armament."

Uxno nodded. "Like what?"

"I've got an Undercarriage-Mounted Resequenced Plasma Disrupter, the fully digital model, complete with instruction manual. And if you send in the proof of purchase, you get a free baseball cap."

"Sweet."

"There's also a Static Telophase Inducer with internal gyroscope. Somebody already made me an offer for that, but I was saving it for you."

"Thank you, Spherical. You have my gratitude, and that of Planet Lirg."

"I'm appropriately pleased," she said. "Now, there's one more thing you might be interested in. It's kind of old, but I think you'll appreciate it." Spherical Mattress Stoyanovich leaned toward the palm-tree aliens, who were still tinkering with the small spaceship. "The boys were salvaging a junked Tyrolean Raider, and they were able to get the Selective Photon Excitement Device running again. I could make you a serious deal for this. I'd even throw in the universal wiring accommodator, so you could hook it into your computer system."

"The Selective Photon Excitement Device? It really works?" Uxno sounded impressed.

"The boys are aces at refitting. Boys, say hello to Uxno and Walter."

The two palm-tree aliens waved their frond-arms and whistled softly.

"You'll have to forgive the boys." The giant thumb glided closer to Uxno and Walter. "They're shy."

"Everyone's life has its difficulties," said Uxno.

Spherical was back to business. "Let's talk retrofitting. How many of these items can I put on your spacecraft today? I could have shown you some engine deionizers, too, but they were stolen by Space Mice from Galaxy Four."

Uxno turned to Walter. "Well, General, what do you think we should do?"

"I don't know," Walter said. "What kinds of weapons do the other flying saucers in the fleet have?"

"Other flying saucers?" Uxno asked. "What other flying saucers?"

"You said there was a fleet."

"I said the *Gilded Excelsior* was the flagship of the fleet. That's true. It is the flagship. It is also the fleet."

"Do you mean to say that you have only *one* spaceship?"

"How many do *you* have?"

"That's not the point!" cried Walter, who was beginning to suspect that he might never see his home or the Video Palace again. "How do you expect to fight the Wotwots with only one ship?"

"Walter," said Uxno, "I suspect that you, being a general, are not concerned with petty details like this, but do you have any idea how expensive a flying saucer is? We have stretched our financial resources to the utmost in preparing this craft for battle. We simply do not have the ready cash to purchase any more and get them in fighting shape."

Walter sighed. "How many ships do the Wotwots have?"

"That's an interesting story—"

At that moment Snartmer came barreling into the room, the feet of his red pajamas skidding across the polished floor.

"Captain!" he shouted. "Come quick!"

6

Uxno, Snartmer, and Walter raced through the space sta-tion's corridors, back toward where the *Gilded Excelsior* was docked.

"We have to leave right away!" Snartmer panted as they ran. "It's the Wotwots! They've gone and done something!"

"What?"

"I was talking to Mong Overthruster at the Spaceline Cafeteria, telling him about how we had taken his advice and gotten a general from Earth."

"And?"

"And he said that he was glad to hear it, because the Wotwots had taken his advice, too!"

"Aarg!" Uxno cried. "Foul destiny has dealt us the two of clubs again! Our one advantage over the terrible Wotwot space armada, and now it's gone! Can't Mong Overthruster keep his mouth shut?"

"Sorry, Captain. Once he gets a good idea, he likes to let as many people as possible know about it."

"Mong Overthruster will get no thanks from Planet Lirg. The rich bounty of the nougat mines will not be his!"

"Once I heard what the Wotwots were up to, I had to think quickly," Snartmer said. "Fortunately, I've been practicing. I rounded up all the crew and told them to get back to the flying saucer and make it ready for immediate departure. I think there's a way we can retain part of our advantage over the Wotwots. Listen: if they've only just now found their general on Earth, they may not yet have built up a good working relationship like the one we have with Walter."

Walter said nothing.

"If we can find them and attack before their general is ready to lead them into battle, victory may still be ours."

"Snartmer! What excellent thinking! When all this is over, I will personally award you the Shiny Gold Star of Honor."

"Thank you, Captain," Snartmer said, genuinely touched.

They had arrived at the *Gilded Excelsior*'s hangar just as Voo, who had been checking the air pressure on the landing gear tires, scampered up the ramp and into the flying saucer.

Uxno examined the spacecraft and nodded approvingly. "It's a shame we weren't able to fit it out with some of Spherical's exotic devices of destruction. We'll just have to make do with our Type A Laser Cannons."

He jogged up the ramp, with Snartmer and Walter following him. "Nevertheless, I suspect that superior generalship is more valuable than superior firepower."

"We still need to talk about this," Walter said. He was having a hard time getting over the fact that their "fleet" was only one flying saucer.

"No time now. We'll talk on the way."

The ramp closed behind them.

On the bridge the crew had taken their seats, and Uxno began shouting out orders. "All stations report in! Begin emergency takeoff procedures—there's no time for the preflight checklist! Pilot, launch this vessel at your most immediate convenience! Your course is already laid in! Hurry!"

The flying saucer darted out of the station and into the dark gulfs of space.

"We're heading for the Erlenmeyer Asteroid Field," Uxno announced to Walter. "This is one of the spots where the Wotwots traditionally sit and lurk. The asteroid field lies right next to one of the intergalactic transit corridors, and the Wotwots like to hide among the asteroids and make rude comments about the designs of the spaceships that pass by. Savages."

Walter wasn't really listening. He couldn't stop thinking about one burning question, and he had to ask it: "How many spaceships do they have?"

"I imagine they will bring whatever they own. Because of their low self-esteem, Wotwots like to travel in groups."

"And how many is that?"

"Voo!" Uxno called. "What are the latest spy reports about the strength of the Wotwot fleet?"

Voo carried her clipboard over to the captain's chair. "At last report, the number of vessels in the Wotwot fleet was . . . one."

"*One?*" Walter shouted, extremely relieved.

Voo scowled. "What's wrong with one?"

"Nothing, it's just that I was afraid it would be something a little, you know, more."

"I'm sorry if we can't manage the kind of space battle that you're used to," Voo said, sounding hurt, "but numbers aren't everything."

"Remember, the Wotwots and Lirgonians have been fighting for three hundred years. The casualties have been staggering," added Snartmer.

"How many ships have you lost?" Walter asked them.

"Two."

"In three hundred years?"

"I told you, the losses have been terrible."

"And the Wotwots?"

"Three."

"You see," Uxno interrupted. "The Wotwots are losing the war! This proves it! And now, with our general, victory is assured!"

"What about their general?" Voo asked glumly.

"Well, Mong Overthruster told me that we got to Earth before the Wotwots did, so we got the first pick and ours should be better."

"Thank you," Walter said. Now that he knew it wasn't going to be the *Gilded Excelsior* against a million Wotwots, he felt a little better.

"But I did get the general's name. Mong Overthruster said the Wotwots were bragging about it on the Long-Range Space Radio just before we arrived."

Walter started to feel worse. He imagined the Wotwots had gotten a fighter pilot or a real army general, not just somebody who had watched a lot of videos.

"Who is it?" Uxno and Voo demanded.

"Yselle Meridian."

Walter turned pale and sank into the white vinyl guest chair.

7

"Walter, are you ill?"

Uxno, Snartmer, and Voo clustered around Walter's chair. The rest of the crew looked on anxiously from their positions.

"Did you trip over something?" asked Voo.

"Are you ill?" Snartmer repeated.

"I know what's wrong," said Uxno. "He's hungry. We should have given him a good meal at Space Station Stoyanovich, but we departed too quickly."

Walter tried to stand up, but Uxno held him down.

"No! Don't exhaust yourself! We will bring you something. Would you care for more tea? We have apple juice as well, but all the muffins have been eaten. I apologize." Uxno turned and shouted at two of the crew members. "Snack Technicians! Bring Walter Nutria some Interstellar Granola Bars!"

"It's all right," Walter insisted, forcing himself out of the chair.

Voo tapped her brother on the shoulder. "That's something I needed to tell you, Uxno. We don't have any more Interstellar Granola Bars. The Space Mice from Galaxy Four were nesting in them, and we had to throw the whole crate out."

"What! Do you realize what you're saying, Voo? Walter Nutria will starve!"

"Really, I'm fine."

"Navigator, where is the nearest Safeway? Emergency velocity!"

Walter waved his arms, desperately trying to get Uxno to pay attention. "I'm not hungry! I'm all right!"

Uxno hesitated. "Really?"

"Really."

"Then why did you fall into the chair?"

"I told you, he tripped."

"Quiet, Voo!"

"It's nothing," Walter said. "I just thought I recognized that name you said."

"You mean Yselle Meridian?"

Uxno pointed. "See! He's turning pale again! Oh, why didn't we bring more food?"

"No, it's all right. But how could the Wotwots have picked Yselle as their general?"

"You know her?" Snartmer asked.

"She's kind of a friend of mine."

"A *girl*friend?" said Voo.

"Woo-OO!" said the rest of the crew in unison.

"Hey!" Uxno raised a warning hand. "It is bad behavior to comment upon our general's social life." Sheepishly, the crew went back to their duties.

"Well, she's not really my girlfriend," Walter said. "I mean,

I don't think so. It's not like we've been out on dates or anything, but we watch movies together all the time." He felt
embarrassed trying to explain all this to the Lirgonians, who
probably didn't care anyway. "Mostly at her house. My mom
doesn't like Yselle very much, so I always say I'm going over to
Timmy Arbogast's or Ezra Bell's, and I go to Yselle's house instead."

Snartmer clapped his red-mittened hands together. "That's
probably how the Wotwots decided to get her as a general.
They checked the records at the video rental store and discovered that you had seen the most movies. Since you were already working for us, they must have taken the next person on
the list—Yselle Meridian."

Walter bit his lip. "I have some bad news about that. Yselle
. . . Yselle's been renting movies with my card."

At this news, Uxno gripped the edge of his captain's chair.
Voo swayed slightly.

"A couple of months ago, Yselle rented *Tarantula*, featuring
John Agar, and didn't bring it back for two weeks. Ever since
then she's been using my video card so she won't have to pay
her overdue charge."

"Do you mean to say that the Wotwots' general has seen
more movies than ours?" Uxno croaked.

"Well . . ."

"Wait! It's all right." Snartmer padded over to Uxno.
"Don't you see, Captain? This demonstrates quick thinking
and a natural ability to solve problems. Instead of being con-
strained by the small-minded rules of the video rental facility,
our general took matters into his own hands and came up
with a solution."

Voo nodded her head, slowly comprehending. "Two people . . . One video rental card . . . Very clever."

"I see your point, Snartmer," Uxno said. "Finding a general with this kind of unorthodox mind is truly a credit to Lirgonian judgment and good taste. The battle will be a mere formality. Victory is assured."

"I don't think you should forget about Yselle."

"Why not?"

Walter looked pained. "Guys, she is *really* smart. She's only a freshman, but she's already taking advanced chemistry."

"Woo-OO," said the rest of the crew.

"Don't you all have jobs?" Uxno reprimanded.

Walter went on. "And she hangs out all the time with the kids who hide behind the football stadium to smoke and play chess."

Uxno's forehead wrinkled. "What are you saying, Walter Nutria?"

"It's just that I'm not sure if I can—"

A *Gilded Excelsior* crew member interrupted this confession. "Captain! We've reached the Erlenmeyer Asteroid Field—and there's a ship in range!"

8

As the *Gilded Excelsior*'s crew scurried to their battle
stations, Walter watched the spaceship approaching on the
viewscreen. The bulky yellow form threaded its way nimbly
through the dense clusters of popcorn ball–shaped asteroids,
and Walter began to tap his foot nervously. At some point the
Lirgonians were going to want him to do something, and Walter was forced to admit to himself that he didn't know how to
do anything. Okay, he could play a pretty decent game of pin-
ball, and he knew about movies, which had gotten him into
this mess in the first place, but that was it. When the battle
started, he could shout out, "Fire all torpedoes!" or "Hard roll
right!" but he didn't know how much good it would do. Despite what the Lirgonians thought, Walter wasn't sure if having seen *Earth Vs. the Flying Saucers* two dozen times really
qualified him to be a space general.

The other ship steadily drew closer, prowling like a fat
metal shark. Walter remembered a maxim that his uncle,
Horton Nutria, was fond of saying: "If you can't do something

properly, at least do it attractively." He folded his arms and tried to look confident.

"Captain, we're in range of the Short-Range Visual Radio," Snartmer called. "Shall I contact them?"

Uxno nodded. "Please do. Ask if they've seen a Wotwot battle cruiser in the vicinity."

So the owners of this sinister-looking craft weren't the dreaded Wotwots after all. Walter unfolded his arms and started to tap his foot again.

"I got through, Captain. I'm putting them on the view-screen now."

The screen revealed the interior of the vessel, which was decorated mostly with shiny chrome and recessed lighting. A skinny creature with green scaly skin and two long antennae sat in the captain's chair.

Uxno cleared his throat purposefully. "Greetings," he announced to the alien on the viewscreen. "This is the *Gilded Excelsior*, flagship of the Planet Lirg battle fleet. Whom do we have the honor of addressing?"

The alien drew his long legs up under himself and began to fidget with the controls in front of him. "This is Orloff Tree aboard the transgalactic cargo ship *Iblis*, and before you ask, we are not smuggling illegal bootleg concert recordings from the Peach Nebula."

"I'm glad to hear it, Captain Orloff Tree—" Uxno began, but Orloff Tree cut him off.

"Oh, I'm not the captain. I'm the swing-shift pilot. Captain Et Cetera is downstairs taking a nap. Do you want me to wake her?" Orloff Tree's antennae bobbed back and forth nervously.

"That won't be necessary, thank you. What I wanted to know was this: have you seen any other spacecraft during this trip through the asteroid field? We're searching for the disreputable Wotwot space armada, and we have reason to believe that they might be in the area."

Orloff Tree's forked tongue protruded as he considered the question. "You know, we haven't exactly seen anyone, but the scanner did pick up some strange readings a little ways back. And there was something on the Long-Range Space Radio, too. We didn't get the entire message, but we heard the words 'bad design' and 'out-of-date color scheme.'"

Uxno leaned forward anxiously. His eyes gleamed with excitement. "It's the Wotwots! No other species in the cosmos is as deliberately rude on a regular basis! Quick, man, where did you hear this?"

"That way." Orloff Tree pointed over his shoulder.

Uxno leaped to his feet. "Pilot, take us that way with all possible and practical speed!"

The *Gilded Excelsior* took off with a jerk, throwing Uxno back into his chair in an undignified heap. "Thank you, Orloff Tree," he called to the fading image on the viewscreen.

"Battle stations!" Uxno shouted. "Remember, it cost a lot of money to train you, and we will pay back the Wotwots in discomfort and ridicule! Walter Nutria, the time is almost at hand! Are you prepared to lead us to victory?"

Walter knew which answer Uxno was looking for.

"Yes."

"Good!"

For a few tense minutes, the flying saucer weaved and dodged through the Erlenmeyer Asteroid Field, always heading in the direction that Orloff Tree had given them. Voo, sitting at the Engineer's Command Console, watched the small green screen of the Local Interesting Material Detector. The Local Interesting Material Detector was the most popular product ever made by the Twin Planets Spacecraft Electronics Corporation. You programmed into it all the things you didn't find interesting, and the detector would ignore all those things and let you know when anything else came into range. It was very helpful for, among other things, finding your way around a new solar system. You told it to ignore "everything except for Planet Miblok," and as soon as something showed up on the screen, you knew it had to be Planet Miblok.

Voo had programmed the Local Interesting Material Detector to ignore the asteroids. Time ticked by, and the screen stayed blank. Voo rubbed a thumb over her stubbly chin and tried to ignore Snartmer, who was sitting in the next seat over, tapping his mittens on the console.

Suddenly, an orange dot began flashing on the outer edge of the detector's screen.

"Uxno!" Voo shouted. "There's something up ahead!"

"What is it?"

"It's not an asteroid."

"Thank you, Voo. We will assume it is the Wotwot spacecraft. Now, Walter Nutria, should we sneak up on our foes or approach boldly, confident in our victory."

Walter shrugged. "Let's be bold."

"Forward, then! Charge up the Type A Laser Cannons. Set destructive potential to 'excessive'!"

Voo's eyes were glued to the detector, which was now flashing madly. "We're getting close. They should be around here somewhere—"

"Look!" Snartmer pointed to the viewscreen. From behind a large asteroid, a spaceship was emerging. It was a long, lean, black-and-silver shape. At one end its rocket engine was surrounded by massive tail fins, and sharp spikes protruded from its nose. Slowly, it turned to face the *Gilded Excelsior*.

The entire crew gasped.

"It's the Wotwots," Uxno said grimly.

9

"Pitiful Lirgonian vessel!" A voice crackled over the *Gilded Excelsior*'s speakers. It sounded like a combination of trash-can lids and dump-truck motors. Once again, Walter instantly envisioned the Wotwots as purple and slimy, with bloodshot bug eyes and segmented exoskeletons.

The voice continued. "Although it is against your nature, we advise you to surrender now. It will save time and whatever dignity you have left—although we have seen your uniforms, and we suspect that you had no dignity to begin with."

"Small words from a small-minded creature. They will be answered with a hail of laser beams." Uxno laughed and thrust out his ample stomach defiantly. Walter wondered if Uxno remembered they were communicating by radio.

"Our new space general," Uxno went on, "will confound your tiny minds, Wotwot! Prepare to shake hands with fear and buy it lunch!"

"Not so fast," replied the grinding, rumbling voice from the Wotwot vessel. "We have a general, too, direct from Earth, and she is very frightening-looking, even to us."

"It does not matter. We got ours first, so it stands to reason that we picked the best one. Ha!"

Walter whispered to Snartmer, "I wish he'd stop saying that."

"It's okay," Snartmer whispered back. "He's just using psychology. Uxno's trying to make the Wotwots feel bad about themselves by pointing out how much smarter we are."

"That's what I mean."

Uxno was still not finished. "And another thing. Your electronics technicians are as lazy and incompetent as the chefs at your so-called Famous Wotwot Hot Dog Stands. Were you aware that the vocal remodulator on your space radio is broken?"

"What?" The *Gilded Excelsior* crew heard a muffled conversation and some clanging noises over the speakers, then the voice returned. "How about this?" it asked. Instead of the harsh, metallic jangle, the voice was now smooth and deep. It reminded Walter of a late-night jazz music show host. "That's better, right?"

"The audio quality has improved somewhat," Uxno said, "but I cannot call it 'better,' since I am still hearing you speak."

"That's it, man! This conversation is over! Now we fight!"

Uxno spun around and stared at Walter. "Well, General, what are your plans?"

"The Wotwot ship is starting to move!" one of the Lirgonian crew members shouted.

Uxno kept staring expectantly at Walter. Walter blinked. He wanted to hide somewhere. For the past several months, his life had consisted mostly of watching movies and pretending to be invisible in school. Now that he was supposed to actually *do* something, he felt overwhelmed.

"Um . . . Activate the tactical computer!" Walter thought he remembered that from *Battle Beyond the Stars*.

"The what?" Voo asked, looking up from her display.

"We don't have one of those," Snartmer whispered to Walter.

"How about going around to the other side? Maybe we can get behind them." Walter had seen that a lot in the movies, and it sounded like a good idea.

The flying saucer took off in its new direction, with the crew working furiously to keep it on course. As they reached the far point of their turn, Snartmer called their attention to the main viewscreen. In the distance they could see that the Wotwot ship, while trying to stay close to the *Gilded Excelsior*, had sideswiped an asteroid and was trying to right itself.

"Now!" Uxno shouted. "While they are disoriented! Fire the Type A Laser Cannons!"

"Wait!" Walter jumped up and stood in front of Uxno. "You can't fire! What about Yselle?"

"What about her? She has joined up with the Wotwots. Not only does this demonstrate a marked lack of taste but it also means she deserves what she gets."

"I don't care." He couldn't just let the Lirgonians open fire—if Yselle got blown up, her parents would be mad at the very least. Also, Walter had been building up his courage for weeks to ask Yselle to the Tulip Extravaganza, East Weston Northside High's annual spring dance. "You can't destroy the Wotwot ship with Yselle on board!"

Uxno turned pale beneath his whiskers. "Walter Nutria! We're not going to destroy anything!"

"Especially with Type A Laser Cannons," added Snartmer.

"One of the key reasons for winning this war is so we can gloat. If we blew them up, the gloating would be rather pointless. I mean to say, who would we gloat at?"

"Well . . ." Walter didn't know what to say to that.

"I'm glad you understand." Uxno pointed to his crew member in charge of the lasers. "Fire!"

Without hesitation the crew member pressed the large red button with the exclamation point on it.

Unfortunately, the crew member in charge of the lasers had been so intent on watching the unfortunate Wotwot battle cruiser that he had forgotten to aim the *Gilded Excelsior*'s Type A Laser Cannons at anything in particular.

Two bolts of crimson light stabbed out of the flying saucer and into a nearby asteroid.

While it was indeed true that these laser beams wouldn't have stopped the Wotwot ship, they were more than enough for the innocent asteroid, which exploded into hundreds of fragments.

By the time the Lirgonians and Walter figured out what had happened, their ship was being hammered by the asteroid fragments and driven seriously off course.

Uxno was nearly in a frenzy. "Voo! Do you have a damage report?"

The ship was wobbling, and Voo had to cling to her console to avoid rolling across the floor. "This is just a guess, but I think we've been hit by a number of asteroid fragments."

"The field of battle is no place for short tempers, Voo. Don't get snippy with me."

"The vessel is stable again, Captain!" Snartmer called. And he was right. It had stopped wobbling.

"Walter Nutria! What are your orders?"

Walter was on the other side of the room, lying in a heap. He had not been as lucky as Voo. The impact of the asteroid fragments had launched him cleanly out of his white vinyl chair. "They might think our ship is disabled," Walter said, crawling to his feet. "Just like in *The Wrath of Khan*. Chase them, while they're not expecting it."

"Here they come!" shouted Snartmer. The Wotwot vessel was large in the viewscreen. "They're firing!" A sparkly round object flew from the side of the Wotwot ship. Walter thought it looked like a wadded-up ball of Christmas tinsel.

Uxno ordered evasive action. "Duck! Get us out of the way!"

The *Gilded Excelsior* spun, narrowly missing the sparkly thing.

"That was a High-Octane Impedance Torpedo," Uxno said, watching the thing pass by. "It will take them time to reload. Now we follow Walter Nutria's advice. Now we give chase!"

10

As the *Gilded Excelsior* twisted and bounced through the Erlenmeyer Asteroid Field, the cases of supplies in the ship's lower deck remained securely tied down.

Except for one.

In a far corner, a box of Auntie Zifnor's All-Natural Mint Cookies rattled gently. Then, with a creaking sound that went completely unnoticed in the hubbub of shouted orders and cursing upstairs, a corner of the box opened.

From the darkness within, two sets of tiny red eyes blinked. Once they were sure no one was paying attention, two small forms emerged from the cookie box. Except for their long, hairless tails, they were covered with electric blue fur that glowed vaguely in the dim light.

They reached the floor and froze, whiskers quivering, ears alert for any sound of danger. They heard none. It was safe.

Scurrying on their silent little feet, the two creatures disappeared among the flying saucer's supplies.

11

The battle had been raging for some time now, and things didn't seem to be going well for either side. The Wotwot ship had a set of scorch marks running down its left side. They were the ugly color of badly burned toast, but there was no real damage. They only reduced the ship's resale value. The Lirgonian flying saucer had been hit as well. There was a large dent on the upper side, the result of not quite getting out of the way of another High-Octane Impedance Torpedo.

Aboard the *Gilded Excelsior*, Walter was learning about the problems of being a general. Those problems were, in one word, Uxno. Although Uxno had personally selected Walter to lead the Lirgonians into battle, he was having a hard time letting Walter give the orders.

Several times Walter had shouted, "Turn around, turn around!" hoping that they might be able to surprise the Wotwots by swinging past a cloud of space dust or a nearby asteroid. But every time they turned away from the Wotwots, Uxno was unable to keep silent. "Fire!" he would shout. "Before they escape! Fire now! Fire a lot!"

After twenty minutes of this, the crew were confused beyond belief. Some of them jumped to action whenever Walter gave an order, some of them waited to hear what Uxno had to say, and a few of them listened to both orders, decided which one sounded better to them, and followed that. Voo sat hunched over the Local Interesting Material Detector, holding her head in her hands.

The *Gilded Excelsior* veered off in a corkscrew motion, firing wildly at everything in the universe, it seemed, except for the Wotwot ship.

"Sorry," Uxno said, for about the dozenth time, as the confused crew drove the flying saucer in the exact wrong direction. "I must be quiet and let our glorious general do his job. I really must."

Walter wanted to say, "Fine—it's your spaceship, you fly it how you want," and let Uxno take over for good, but he didn't. Now that he was here, Walter was starting to feel responsible for the Lirgonians who had put him in charge. He wanted to try to do his best for them, and he knew if he let Uxno drive, they would probably end up running into an asteroid or getting lost in a nebula someplace.

Walter reassured the captain. "It's all right, Uxno. We'll get it right next time."

Besides, the Wotwots didn't seem to be doing any better. Whereas the Lirgonians seemed to be constantly zooming off in the wrong direction, the Wotwots were having a hard time picking a direction at all. They would go forward, then stop suddenly, then cruise backward for a while, then spin a little and go forward again. Perhaps Yselle and the Wotwot captain were having the same problems as Walter and Uxno.

A little bit later, it was clear that the Wotwots had gotten things organized before Walter and the Lirgonians. Their rocket ship had maneuvered behind the *Gilded Excelsior* and was pursuing it doggedly. Soon, the Wotwots would be close enough to use their High-Octane Impedance Torpedoes again, or maybe something even worse.

Uxno sat rigid in his captain's chair, mittened hands clamped over his mouth, trying to be good.

Walter stared nervously at the rearview viewscreen. Time was running out.

Suddenly, he had a thought. "Snartmer, how fast can this flying saucer stop?"

Snartmer dug under his seat and pulled out a plastic notebook with GILDED EXCELSIOR—OFFICIAL TECHNICAL DATA embossed on the cover in gold letters. He flipped through the pages, scanning the columns of figures and data. "Very fast," Snartmer said, finding the correct information.

"Great. Voo, I want you to get ready to stop. When I say so, throw on the brakes, or the retro-rockets, or whatever."

Voo reached up to grab an orange-striped lever. "All set."

Uxno could contain himself no longer. "I comprehend! When the Wotwots get close enough, we stop, and they fly right past us. We'll have them for sure!"

"That's right," Walter said. This was something he had seen in *Top Gun*, and he hoped it would work the same way in outer space. The Wotwot spacecraft filled the entire rearview viewscreen now, its long, narrow form getting closer and closer like a sinister mechanical pencil. "When can they use their torpedoes?"

Voo checked her readouts. "Actually, they could use them anytime now. They've been in range for the past couple of—"

"It doesn't matter!" Walter shouted. "Stop now! Pull the lever!"

Voo pulled the lever.

There was an earsplitting screech, exactly like the engine block of a 1949 Packard seizing up. The entire flying saucer vibrated, and the crew strained forward in their trauma harnesses. Except for Walter, who had no trauma harness. He skidded out of his chair again and hit the stainless-steel floor with a thump.

"We did it!" Snartmer shouted above the noise. "We're slowing down! The Wotwot ship is going too fast! They're going to pass us by! We've got them! We—"

Snartmer was interrupted by the Wotwot ship running into them. The Wotwots were so close behind the *Gilded Excelsior* that, when it stopped suddenly, they had no time to react. The nose of their ship plowed into the flying saucer with a sickening impact that tested the Lirgonians' trauma harnesses to the maximum degree. On the floor, Walter clutched the base of Uxno's chair to keep from ping-ponging across the room.

When the chaos had subsided a little, Uxno tried to make himself heard over the babble of panicked voices and grinding metal. "Voo! Voo! Where are the Wotwots? Are they ahead of us?"

The lights were flickering on and off, and the big viewscreens had all gone out. Voo leaned close to her glowing green readouts and squinted. "I'm not sure . . . Wait a second . . . Uxno! Walter Nutria! Take a look at this!"

"What is it?" Uxno scampered quickly to Voo's side while Walter pulled himself up from the floor.

"Are the Wotwots in front of us?" Uxno asked again.

Voo shook her head. "Not exactly."

Walter tried to make sense of the flashing blobs of light on Voo's sensors. "Are they behind us?"

"They're not behind us, either."

Uxno frowned. "Voo, I appreciate your linguistic precision, but now is the time for plain answers, and fast ones. Where are they?"

"They're right on top of us. We're stuck together."

12

"**Attention, Wotwot vessel! Attention, Wotwot vessel! This is** the *Gilded Excelsior*. Do you copy?"

Voo repeated her message into the Short-Range Space Radio while Uxno paced back and forth in tight circles.

"Can't we do anything?" Uxno fretted. "What about the Type A Laser Cannons? Can't we blast them off?"

Snartmer was running from console to console, helping the rest of the crew get their stations back on-line. "Sorry, Captain, but they seem to have run directly into the lasers' gyroscopic housing. We can't shoot anything."

"Unarmed? Oh, the indignity! The Executive Committee of Planet Lirg will sneer at us! Our bonuses will be reduced for this, have no doubt!"

Snartmer had gotten the lights working again, as well as some of the equipment. Walter studied the reactivated viewscreen. It was focused on the twisted mass of metal where the two spacecraft were locked together. "It looks like they ran into us with their torpedo-launcher thingy. Maybe they can't fire either," he said.

This didn't make Uxno feel any better. "Oh, anguish! Our hated foes are at their most defenseless, and we are unable to act! But wait!" He stopped pacing. "Quickly, someone get me a space suit and a fire ax! We'll take care of these Wotwots the old-fashioned way!"

Voo ignored Uxno and went back to the radio. "Attention, Wotwot vessel! Attention, Wotwot vessel! This is the *Gilded Excelsior*. Do you copy?"

This time, there was an answer.

"Lirgonian vessel *Gilded Excelsior*, this is the WSS *Ferlinghetti*. We can hear you." There was a pause. "We just don't want to talk to you."

Uxno pointed to the radio speakers. "See! Their manners are as bad as their navigation skills! It is time to put some distance between us and them. Drive on!"

Voo started to protest, but Uxno cut her off. "Forward! Our momentum will separate the two ships! Go!"

The engines whined and the *Gilded Excelsior* shuddered. For a second it looked as if they were going to pull away. Then there was a giant bang from somewhere below the floor, and everything stopped.

"I told you so," Voo said. "Engine overload."

While this was going on, Walter noticed that there were still sounds coming from the Short-Range Space Radio's speakers. He heard muffled grunts and clatterings, and something that sounded like angry whispers back and forth. Finally, a voice came back on: "*Gilded Excelsior*, this is the WSS *Ferlinghetti* again."

It was another voice, not the smooth baritone that the

Wotwots had used before. Walter recognized this voice. "Yselle!" he cried.

"Gilded Excelsior, we *do* want to talk to you!"

"No, we don't!" That was the Wotwot's voice, coming from somewhere behind Yselle.

"Yes, we do!"

Walter ran to the microphone, nearly tripping over Snartmer, who was lying on his back trying to fix a smashed console. He snatched the microphone out of Voo's hands. "Yselle!"

"Walter, is that you?"

"Yes! It is! It's me! I'm here!"

"They told me that the Lirgonians may have gotten you. Are you all right?"

"I'm fine," Walter said. Then he stopped. It was always this way—when they weren't watching movies or playing video games, he never knew what to say to Yselle. Whatever he tried always came out sounding stupid. Finally, he asked, "How did you get here?"

"Well, I was in the middle of my piano lesson at Mrs. Olafson's house, and her phone rang. She got up to answer it, and when she got back she looked all pale. It was my dad, she said. My great-aunt Matilda had been rushed to the hospital for an emergency ingrown toenail operation, and my family was sending a car to pick me up."

"I didn't know you had a great-aunt Matilda," Walter said.

"I don't. But it was either play along or go back to Minuet in G Minor for the millionth time."

"Good choice."

"That's just like the Wotwots," Snartmer said. "Cheap theatrics and unnecessary drama."

Walter shushed him.

Yselle continued. "So I went out and sat on the front steps. There wasn't any car, but I noticed this rope ladder hanging down over the side of the porch. When I looked up I saw that it was attached to the Wotwot rocket ship, which was hovering over Mrs. Olafson's house. I thought, Why not? and climbed up."

"The Short-Range Visual Radio is working," Voo announced to no one in particular. "We can open up visual communications now."

"Sunglasses out!" Uxno ordered. Instantly, each member of the crew reached into the pocket of their red pajamas, pulled out a pair of thick black sunglasses, and put them on.

Walter stared at the spectacle.

"This is for protection, Walter Nutria," Uxno explained. "The Wotwots are not the worst prom dates in the universe just because of their bad personalities. The Wotwots are singularly unattractive creatures. One glance is often enough to cause massive internal injuries and acute psychological distress."

"I heard that!" shouted the Wotwot captain. "Coming from a species that only has one outfit, we consider your disgust a compliment!"

"It's good that you do," said Uxno. "It's the only kind of compliment you're likely to get."

"Will you both stop it, please!" It was Yselle, who had wrestled the microphone away from the Wotwot captain again.

Uxno wasn't listening. "Before we establish visual communications, our general must be protected from such high-dosage ugliness. Someone run down to the Auxiliary Sunglasses Storage Locker and get a pair for Walter Nutria."

"Will you pay attention to me!" Yselle shouted into the radio. "We can't use visual communications. The Short-Range Video whatever-it-is is missing."

Uxno raised an eyebrow. "Missing?"

"Yeah. They said it was stolen by Space Mice from Galaxy Four."

To his credit, Uxno resisted making a snide remark. That was just as well, since Walter was about to remind Uxno of the *Gilded Excelsior*'s own Space Mouse problems.

"I don't know how we're going to get these ships unstuck. Have you tried your engines yet?" asked Yselle. "Do they work?"

Walter reached for the microphone.

"Walter Nutria!" Uxno shouted. "What are you doing? Don't give out secret tactical information to the enemy!" Even Snartmer and Voo looked on with expressions of shock.

"Guys, listen. We can't go anywhere. Our ships are locked together, and we're floating around in the middle of this asteroid field. We're going to have to cooperate with the Wotwots on this. What else are we supposed to do?"

"We'll think of something!" Uxno replied.

"We always think of something," said Voo.

"Well, we usually think of something," added Snartmer.

"Go ahead, then," said Walter. "Think of something." He folded his arms and waited. After a minute of silence, he said, "Well?"

"Give us more time!" Uxno demanded.

"It usually takes a while," added Snartmer.

Walter shook his head. "I know you aren't going to like this, but we're going to be stuck here forever if we don't figure something out. And that means talking to Yselle and the Wotwots."

At this suggestion, the Lirgonians muttered and grumbled and tried not to make eye contact with Walter.

"Guys, you made me your general, didn't you? Well, either you did that because you thought I could help or you're all completely nuts. If you're not nuts, then I think you should listen to me."

Voo and Snartmer looked at the ground shamefacedly. Uxno scuffed his pajama foot across the floor and mumbled.

"What was that?" Walter asked.

"Fine," Uxno said, still sulking.

Walter picked up the microphone again. "Yselle, are you there?"

"Still waiting, Walter."

"Great. Our engines can't move us anywhere. We tried, but they overloaded and shut themselves down. What about yours?"

"The same. I have an idea, though. What if we both switched on our engines at the same time? Together, they might have enough power to move both ships."

"That sounds good." Walter turned to the *Gilded Excelsior*'s crew. "What about it?" he asked. "Do you think that would work?"

Voo dropped into her engineer's chair. "It might," she said grouchily.

"All right. Get ready." To Yselle, he said, "What about you? Are the Wotwots ready to try?"

There was some silence over the radio, then Yselle came back on. "They're not happy about it, but they'll try."

"Everybody ready, then? On the count of three . . ."

"One," said Yselle Meridian.

"Two," said Walter Nutria.

"Three," said the two space generals together.

Voo pressed the button that read ENGINES GO NOW. In the WSS *Ferlinghetti*'s engineering cubicle, the Wotwot driver pushed his speed throttle up to WAY FAST.

The noise of the two engines got louder and louder, and the ships started shaking like an unsafe ride at the county fair. As the noise and vibration built up, Walter wondered if the ships' engines were even pointing in the same direction.

Then, with a motion so small he barely noticed it at first, the locked-together space vessels started to go forward.

"Hey!" Voo pointed her mitten at a row of gauges. "Look! We're moving!"

Walter watched the floating asteroids slide gently past the viewscreen. "We're moving! We did it!"

"Yay!" Uxno cried. "Another triumph for Walter Nutria and Planet Lirg. Nothing can defeat us—not battle, not misfortune, not even cooperation!"

13

The *Gilded Excelsior*, flagship of the Lirgonian battle fleet, had two circular decks, one on top of the other. The top deck was the Command Deck, where all the important things happened. Underneath that was the Supply Deck, a much larger open area that was usually filled with rickety metal shelves and rows of crates.

Like the Wotwots themselves, the Wotwot spacecraft was designed in a vastly different way. Instead of having a few main decks, the WSS *Ferlinghetti* was set up in compartments. These small rooms, hundreds of them separated by beaded curtains, were only as large as they had to be, and not a bit larger. The Drive Room, where the Wotwot captain commanded the vessel, was big enough to hold exactly four Wotwot officers. There was no elbow room at all, which was fine, since the Wotwots had no elbows.

Once Yselle Meridian had been taken aboard and convinced to become their general, the Second-Chair Navigator had to give up his seat so that Yselle wouldn't have to fight the entire war standing up. Then, because there was no more space, he had to run all the way to Room 24B–Theta 6 at the other end of the rocket ship, grab an Intergalactic Lawn Chair, and sit in the hall outside the Drive Room.

This all may sound like a pain, but the Wotwots liked it. They liked to keep things in compartments. That way, they knew exactly where to find something whenever they wanted it. The Lirgonians thought the Wotwots were compulsive neat-freaks. The Wotwots thought the Lirgonians were slobs.

The Wotwots' compartment system was also a benefit to the pair of tiny, long-tailed, blue-furred creatures that lived in Subchamber X-42–Left-Side Purple. Subchamber X-42–Left-Side Purple was where the Wotwots kept their guitar strings and lemon-flavored cough drops. No one aboard the WSS *Ferlinghetti* had popped a string or come down with a sniffle in weeks, so the creatures' nest had been safe as they scouted the ship. They had explored every one of the hundreds of compartments on the Wotwot vessel, and they had scurried across every inch of the thickly carpeted corridors. They saw everything. Yselle Meridian's arrival and the desperate battle with the Lirgonians had not gone unnoticed by their beady eyes and little round ears.

Now they crouched on the floor of Subchamber X-42–Left-Side Purple, their pink noses almost touching, their whiskers quivering, squeaking softly back and forth to each other. They were planning their next move.

It was almost time to act, but not quite. They didn't mind waiting. The Space Mice from Galaxy Four were patient.

14

The *Gilded Excelsior* and the WSS *Ferlinghetti* struggled gracelessly out of the Erlenmeyer Asteroid Field and on through deep space. They were moving now, but that solved only half the problem. Assuming that the Wotwots and the Lirgonians didn't want to spend the rest of eternity with their two flagships stuck together, they needed to get them separated.

At first they had hoped it would be possible just to pry the spaceships apart with crowbars or Plasma-Infused Tire Irons. A low-ranking Lirgonian, Extremely Petty Officer Third Class Paff, was sent out in a space suit and magnetic boots to examine the damage. When EPOTC Paff returned, stamping his feet and shivering with cold, his report was not good. The ships had crunched together like nobody's business. The Stroboscopic Integrity Coordinator on the *Gilded Excelsior* had been speared right through by a piece of metal from the Wotwot ship, and that delicate instrument would probably be ripped out if they tried to get the ships apart. And, as everyone knows, operating a spacecraft without a Stroboscopic Integrity Coordinator is complete madness. EPOTC Paff admitted that he didn't know much about Wotwot spaceships, but he didn't think the WSS *Ferlinghetti* had gotten off any easier. The *Gilded Excelsior*'s Type A Laser Cannons had torn a long hole in the side of the Wotwot rocket engine, and EPOTC Paff had seen a bunch of shredded plastic tubing and sparking wires inside the gash.

It was clear that they had to get to a garage, and quickly. But which one? Under no circumstances would the Lirgonians agree to go to Wotwot. The Wotwots held the same attitude about Lirg. Space Station Stoyanovich was out of the question as well. Spherical Mattress Stoyanovich would laugh herself sick at the sight of them, and Mong Overthruster, who had nothing better to do than hang around the Spaceline Cafeteria and gossip all the time, would make sure that everyone in the known cosmos heard about what had happened.

The Wotwots suggested heading for the nearest Trans-Galactic Bodywork and Guaranteed 20-Minute Oil Change Station. This would have been fine, except that the Wotwot captain made the mistake of mentioning that he needed only one more stamp on his Trans-Galactic Frequent Customer Card to get 15 percent off on his next visit. Knowing this, the Lirgonians refused to go there. "It is highly offensive, not to mention a bad idea, to help the leader of the dreaded Wotwot space armada save a little cash," said Uxno. "Forget it."

"How about Space Station Omelet-7?" Snartmer suggested.

"It got two and a half stars in the latest issue of *Deep Space*

Freight Hauler magazine," said Uxno. "And we all know it employs some of the best mechanics in the Pale Pink Star Cluster."

The Wotwots refused on general principle, still annoyed that the Lirgonians had shot down their first choice.

This kind of bickering went on for a very long time as the locked-together ships crawled through interstellar space. While they had no specific destination, they tried to avoid the high-traffic areas and star systems where they knew anyone. The fewer space travelers who found out about this, the better.

The arguments went on long enough for Walter to have some tea and take a nap. Much later, someone suggested Jerry & Mo's Spacecraft Repair Plaza on Ice Planet B. There was a minute of stunned silence.

It was an obvious solution, and both the Lirgonians and the Wotwots were amazed that it had taken hours on end to think of. Ice Planet B was far outside the normal territories of both groups, and the mechanics at Jerry & Mo's were known to do good work and keep their mouths shut (those who had mouths).

Both sides agreed at once. Almost immediately, both sides tried to take credit for suggesting it in the first place. Gracelessly, the two ships made a wide, staggering turn in the direction of the Hopkins Galaxy and Ice Planet B.

As they zoomed toward their destination, Walter Nutria sat on the Command Deck of the *Gilded Excelsior* and finished his second cup of tea. While Uxno was on the other side of the room, arguing with Voo over some minor repairs, Snartmer occupied the captain's chair. Unlike Snartmer's own chair,

Uxno's could spin all the way around. Snartmer loved this, and sat in Uxno's chair whenever he could get away with it.

"Ice Planet B's not a place we visit a lot," Snartmer explained to Walter, "because it's pretty far away from the major intergalactic nougat processing centers. Almost everyone else does, though. It's a great planet to go shopping. There are stores from almost everywhere in the known universe on Ice Planet B. And they have free gift wrap. It's the law. The Wotwots don't go there because they hate malls. They're too snooty to be seen at a food court."

"I heard that!" said the Wotwot captain over the radio, which had been left on. "We stay away from Ice Planet B because malls are square. There is no spiritual fulfillment in a mall. Besides, we shop by mail order. It's just easier."

Walter didn't want to listen to yet another argument over nothing, so he changed the subject as fast as he could. "Is it really cold on this planet?"

Snartmer sighed. "Yes, it really is. Unlike that of Planet Tropica, Ice Planet B's name is not just a cruel joke on the tourists. In fact, I checked the weather report, and it gave a hundred percent chance of snow, with levels ranging from 'moderately annoying' to 'a real pain.' You don't have a warmer coat, do you?"

"Sorry."

"We'll have to get you one from our supplies. At least we're not going to Ice Planet A. That one's *really* cold."

In time, a small gray disk appeared on the viewscreen.

"Is that Ice Planet B?" Walter asked.

"You bet your feet it is."

"Associate Captain Snartmer?" Uxno had snuck up behind them without making any noise. Snartmer, startled, spun the chair around to face him.

"Yes, Captain?"

"Get out of my chair."

Snartmer leaped up, and Uxno took his place. "Attention, crew," he announced. "We are now approaching our destination, so prepare for landing procedures. I think we all know what kinds of mistakes can happen when trying to land a single space vessel, let alone two of them together. For that reason I want you to . . ." Uxno hesitated. "I want you to co-ordinate with the Wotwots. Is that understood?"

All around the *Gilded Excelsior*, the little red hoods on the Lirgonian space pajamas nodded.

"Fine. Everyone check your trauma harnesses."

Walter was used to this by now. He gripped the armrests of his chair and closed his eyes.

As they approached the planet, the Lirgonians shouted back and forth to each other, as well as to the Wotwots over the radio. Miraculously, there were no arguments this time. They entered the atmosphere, and the flying saucer started to shake and lurch. At one point there was a long, screeching, metal-tearing sound that made Walter hold his breath, but everything held together. Before they realized it, the two space vehicles had settled gently onto the landing field of Jerry & Mo's Spacecraft Repair Plaza.

Uxno stood up. "Crew, pat yourselves on the back. You made a perfect landing under difficult conditions. Rest assured that this will be noted in your performance evaluations. Voo, Snartmer, Walter Nutria, and I will go find Jerry and Mo. Then we can work on getting our two craft separated. Someone run down to the supply deck and retrieve the parkas."

The radio speaker crackled. "We'll meet you out there," said the Wotwot captain.

15

Snartmer hadn't been kidding about the weather report. As Walter, wrapped in a heavy-duty Lirgonian parka, trudged down the *Gilded Excelsior*'s stairs, snow was falling so heavily that he could hardly see fifty feet in front of him. The two spaceships had touched down in the middle of Jerry and Mo's landing field, a giant bowl-shaped area surrounded by tall curving walls. Other space vehicles stood around close by. Some of them had tarps pitched over them, sheltering the mechanics who were working busily with blowtorches and huge wrenches.

Walter looked back at the ships that had just landed. The *Gilded Excelsior* leaned on two of its three landing feet, the third sticking up in the air. The WSS *Ferlinghetti* rested unsteadily on one of its tail fins. An exit ramp was barely visible at the far end of the Wotwot ship. He thought he saw a blond-haired figure walking down the ramp, followed by several large dark shapes.

With a twinge of excitement, Walter realized that he was about to see the Wotwots for the first time.

Uxno, Snartmer, Voo, and Walter plodded across the landing field, leaning into the wind. They were headed for a red neon sign that read LOBBY—THIS WAY, with an arrow underneath pointing to a door with a window in it. Through the window was a brightly lit room. They hurried.

Inside the lobby it was warm. It smelled like motor oil and hot engines. Along the walls were couches made from the seats of old deep-space freighters. A hot-water urn simmered quietly in the corner.

Voo unzipped her parka. "Nice place. I wonder where Jerry and Mo are. You'd think that one of them would be around."

Across the lobby, another door opened.

"Yselle!" Walter shouted.

"Hi, Walter."

Yselle was wrapped up in her old police jacket and looked half frozen.

Walter didn't know what to say again, so he asked the obvious question: "Are you all right?"

"More or less," she said. "What about you? I heard—" Yselle stopped when she noticed that Walter wasn't paying attention anymore. He was staring at what had appeared in the doorway behind her.

Walter took a step backward. Behind him, he heard Uxno say, "So, we meet again!"

The creature that had entered the room was nearly as large as a Volkswagen Beetle. It was nearly the same shape, too, if you turned the Beetle upside down. Its skin was lumpy, with the color and texture of a potato. It walked around on long, stringy tentacles that sprouted from its underside and wore a red-and-gold knitted sock on the end of each tentacle. There was no head (or arms or legs, for that matter).

Walter saw two beady eyes and a small mouth set in the creature's side. Below the mouth was a neat, triangular, mossy beard. A second creature followed the first into the lobby. Walter noticed that they both had beards.

"Walter," Yselle said, "I'd like you to meet Fip, captain of the WSS *Ferlinghetti*, and Burkhardt, his backup. Notice anything?"

Walter nodded. "Yeah. They look just like giant rutabagas."

"Hey!" Burkhardt pointed a quivering tentacle at Walter. "Listen up, Daddy-o! Rutabagas look like *us*, not the other way around!"

"Sorry."

"It's okay, I made that mistake, too," Yselle said. "I meant their little socks. They're the same as our school colors."

"Oh, I see. Now that you mention it, that is kind of strange."

"Stay cool. It's a complete coincidence," Fip said. "Although if you've been hanging out with the Lirgonians, you're probably used to all kinds of goofy stuff."

As strange as it was to hear that rich voice coming from what looked like a giant vegetable, Walter was quickly getting used to it. He introduced Yselle to Uxno, Snartmer, and Voo, praying that they would not mention the word *girlfriend*. They didn't.

"I know they all kind of look alike," Walter whispered to Yselle while hanging up his parka, "but don't say anything. They're a little sensitive about it. You learn to tell them apart pretty fast."

Meanwhile, the Lirgonians and the Wotwots stood staring at each other.

"Since we're all getting to know everyone, Fip, why don't you tell Walter Nutria your full name?" asked Uxno, with a smirk.

"I already did. It's Fip."

"Your *full* name."

Fip glanced over in the direction of Yselle and Walter.

"You never told me you had another name," Yselle said.

"It's Fip Twangler."

"Your *full* full name," Uxno prompted.

Fip glared at him. If Fip didn't reveal it, Uxno certainly would. Uxno grinned. Fip glared some more.

"Fip Twangler Multifarious Prabang Clavicle," he said finally.

The Lirgonians burst into laughter, and the Wotwots shuffled menacingly forward. Immediately Walter and Yselle got between the two groups.

"You see!" Burkhardt pointed at the Lirgonians, who were just beginning to recover. "It's no wonder we're at war all the time. Show them a fairly sharp name like Fip's, and look what happens! No culture! No sense of what's hip!"

"Uncultured? Look at those socks!" Uxno said. "They're probably acrylic!"

"In a second, you're going to get a pretty close look when they stomp all over your little head."

"That's enough!" Yselle pushed Fip and Uxno apart. "This is precisely the reason we're here at this garage in the first place! What is wrong with you two?"

"Uxno and Fip have a history of bad blood," said Snartmer.

"What?"

"Well, it started a long time ago, back when they were on the same basketball team—"

"That'll be enough out of you, Snartmer," said Uxno, threateningly.

"Exactly," Fip agreed, frowning at Snartmer.

They were prevented from going deeper into this subject by the front door flying open. Two aliens hustled in, shivering from the cold. One of them looked like a giant lizard, six feet tall and covered in pink-and-silver fur instead of scales. The other was an ornate Victorian bookcase, with quivering antennae above the molding. In fact, these were the owners of the garage, Jerry and Maureen (known to friends as Mo).

Although Walter and Yselle had no way of knowing this, Jerry was a member of this planet's native species, the modest and industrious Snow Lizards of Ice Planet B. In an attempt to stay out of the perpetual freezing cold of Ice Planet B, the Snow Lizards were the first culture to develop a working mall, complete with extensive parking facilities and food court. An equally notable Snow Lizard contribution to cosmic civilization was their successful introduction of the forward pass to the official rules of intergalactic football.

Jerry's wife, Maureen, was from the Bookshelf Tribe of the Upper Esophageal Star Cluster. Despite having no hands or tentacles to make their own books, the Bookshelf Tribe was one of the most well-read communities in all the galaxies. This was accomplished by sneaking into the libraries of other cultures, posing as, obviously, bookshelves, and subsequently being filled with books by unsuspecting librarians. Through a miracle of adaptive evolution, they were able to absorb the contents of the books directly into their nervous systems by osmosis. In this way, the aliens could methodically digest the entire stored knowledge of any planet they visited.

"Sorry we were away," said Jerry, shaking like a wet sheepdog to clear the melting snow out of his fur. "We had to pick up some fan belts. Now, what can we do for you?"

Voo pointed out through the window to the landing field. "See those two ships out there?"

Mo's antennae bent in that direction. "What in the name of the twin moons of Pentax XII happened to them? They look like they ran into each other!" Mo sounded like the Queen of England, exactly the kind of voice a Victorian bookcase ought to have.

"Well . . ." Voo glanced nervously at Uxno. Uxno raised his eyebrows at Fip. Fip squinted back. Even on Ice Planet B, where no one knew who they were, none of them felt like telling the embarrassing story of the space battle.

The uncomfortable silence started to stretch out.

Yselle finally spoke. "There was . . ." she started to say but immediately ran out of inspiration.

". . . an accident!" Walter finished. "A giant space . . ."

". . . cow," Yselle added.

"Ran out in front of us."

"We both swerved, and . . ."

". . . we ended up hitting each other."

"But we missed the cow."

From opposite sides of the room, Uxno and Fip nodded at each other. It was clear they had chosen the right people for their generals.

"A cow?" Jerry said slowly.

The Lirgonians and Wotwots were quick to agree.

"It was a cow. A space cow."

"Biggest space cow I ever saw."

"It just came out of nowhere. You know what space cows are like."

"Well, you folks aren't the first to come in here with space-cow damage," Jerry said, pulling tools off their places on the walls and stacking them on Mo's shelves. "Let's go take a look and see how bad the damage is."

16

The falling snow had developed into a real snowstorm, hiding nearly everything from view, except for the flashing yellow lights on the snowplows. Snowplows were a fixture on Ice Planet B, and they had been specially designed to always be visible. No one wants to run into a snowplow unexpectedly.

Through this storm, a ragged clump of figures trudged. The Lirgonians were on one side, the Wotwots on the other, and Walter and Yselle in the middle. Even though the aliens were starting to get along better, Walter and Yselle still tried to stay between them as much as possible.

No one spoke much. The humans were too cold, and the aliens were too annoyed.

After a long wait in the lobby of Jerry & Mo's, Jerry had returned from the landing field to report on what he had found. The Snow Lizard had tried to keep a straight face, but it was obvious that he didn't believe their giant space-cow story as much as he had at first. But whatever the cause, the damage was bad. Jerry would have to use his Power-Assisted Multi-Phase Industrial-Size Block and Tackle to pull the two ships apart. Then he, Mo, and their expert staff of trained technicians would have to begin extensive repairs.

The good news was that neither the WSS *Ferlinghetti* nor the *Gilded Excelsior* was totaled. They could, in fact, fix everything. Jerry and Mo even had all the necessary parts in stock. Unfortunately, the repairs would take at least a couple of days. Despite Uxno's and Fip's offers, Jerry did not need the crew of either vessel to hang around and help with the repairs. Although he didn't say this, Jerry had seen what the Wotwots and Lirgonians had done to their own ships, and he was frightened at the thought of having dozens of them running loose in his garage.

So the two humans and the high-ranking Lirgonians and Wotwots had gone to find a place to stay. Mo had mentioned that there were some hotels a few blocks away, attached to the Ice Planet B Convention Center, so they walked, grumbling and snow-covered, in that direction.

The first place they found was a branch of the well-known Interplanetary Diamond Hotel chain. A heated escalator carried them from the sidewalk up to the front door, and they hurried out of the cold and into a vast, two-story atrium. It was full of potted ferns and palm trees, luxuriantly green despite the blizzard raging outside. Walter wondered if any of the palm trees were actually aliens like those who worked for

Spherical Mattress Stoyanovich. Next to the elevators there was a grand piano. A being that looked like a combination musk ox and snail was playing it.

Fip listened to the tune for a second, then winced. "He's playing 'Night and Day' way too fast," he announced.

"I like it here," Uxno said, looking around. "This will be the place where we stay."

Fip disapproved. If he'd possessed a head, he would have shaken it. "No way. It's too . . . What's the word I'm looking for?"

"Pretentious? Bourgeois? Nowheresville?" suggested Burkhardt, his backup.

"Exactly. All these Interplanetary Diamond hovering hotels are just the same. A bunch of fake antiques and ugly little blazers for the staff."

"I think it has dignity," Uxno said. "I think it has character. An appropriate bearing."

"You would."

"Shut up."

"You shut up!"

"All right!" Yselle shouted. "That's enough. If you two don't cut it out, Walter and I are going to go home, then you can sort out your problems by yourselves. And I think you both know how successful that's going to be."

Since they were stranded on a frozen planet in the middle of another galaxy, Walter wondered exactly how Yselle was going to make good on that threat. But it seemed to make Uxno and Fip behave. They looked embarrassed and shuffled their feet and tentacles, respectively.

"Your point is taken," Uxno mumbled. "Sorry."

"Yeah. We'll stop," said Fip.

Walter tried to help Yselle out. He folded his arms and attempted to look stern. "Good," he said. "Now before you start fighting again, why don't you go see if this hotel has enough room for everyone?"

Fortunately, it did. It took a little more argument, but in the end both groups agreed to stay. The Lirgonians stayed because they appreciated the hotel, and the Wotwots stayed because they could make fun of it.

The Interplanetary Diamond Hotel was a full-service hotel, and it had antigravity shuttle buses, complete with extra-strong heaters, available to ferry the crews of the two space-ships over from the garage. Fip and Burkhardt, and Uxno, Snartmer, and Voo, went with the buses, to give directions and explain things to their crews.

"Do you think it was a good idea to let them go by themselves?" Yselle asked, as the whine of the two flying buses faded into the snow-muffling distance.

"Probably. Well, maybe. I hope so. I think they'll try to be good, at least for a little while. You really scared them by threatening to quit," said Walter. "What did the Wotwots promise you in order to get you to work for them?"

"A Hammond B-3 organ and a giant bag of gold."

"Not bad. I got a year's worth of profit from the Lirgonians' nougat mines."

"*Nougat* mines?"

"Haven't you heard of the Lirgonian nougat mines? Those guys are the nougat kings of the universe, so they tell me."

78

"Most of the Wotwots make their living in the recording industry. Except, of course, for the members of the mighty Wotwot space armada. Some of them are professional poets, too. If we survive all this, I'll have to show you some of the Wotwot poetry they read me. It's freaky, but cool. They say they were influenced by the Beat poets, back on Earth. You know, Jack Kerouac and Gary Snyder, guys like that."

Walter laughed. "Giant beatnik rutabagas?" That image, and the fact that it was actually true, struck Walter as unbelievably funny. Pretty soon, Yselle was laughing, too. One of the piano player's multiple eyes glanced disapprovingly in their direction. Walter and Yselle hid behind the ferns until they got their giggling back under control.

"You know what? This is still a lot better than school," Walter said, wiping his eyes.

"If this hadn't happened, I would have been . . ." Yselle trailed off.

"What?"

Yselle didn't say anything. She kept staring out across the atrium to the reception desk.

"Hello, General Meridian?" Walter prompted. No answer.

Yselle pointed to the reception desk, where someone was checking in. "Isn't that Debbie Cromwell?"

Walter squinted over at the person, who was standing next to a pile of luggage. "I don't believe it. You're right. What's she doing here?"

Debbie Cromwell was the most popular girl at East Weston Northside High. She was a cheerleader and captain of the karate team, and she had the second highest grade-point average in the entire school. Everyone knew she was going to become a doctor and cure some really important disease. The teachers loved her.

Yselle couldn't stand Debbie Cromwell.

"I think that *is* Debbie. Weird, huh?" Walter turned back to face Yselle. This was the first conversation he'd had with her where they weren't talking about movies and Walter wasn't fumbling for words. He wasn't about to let a little thing like Debbie Cromwell get in the way.

Yselle kept staring over Walter's shoulder. "Oh, great. She sees us. She's waving. She's coming over."

Reluctantly, Walter and Yselle emerged from the foliage as Debbie Cromwell glided across the atrium. Debbie waved again. "Walter, is that you?"

"Hi, Debbie." Walter and Debbie were in the same economics class. Walter sat to Debbie's left, and when no one was looking he copied her notes.

"And you're Yselle Meridian, right? We're in Drama Club together."

" 'Lo." Yselle stared down at her sneakers.

Debbie put her hands on her hips and looked at both of them. "Whatever are you two doing here?"

Walter started to tell her about the stainless-steel flying saucer and the giant Wotwot rocket ship that had appeared over East Weston and carried them away on this adventure, but he stopped. "It's a long story," he said instead.

"What about you?" Yselle asked Debbie. She couldn't imagine that Debbie Cromwell had watched enough movies to qualify as an intergalactic general for anybody.

Debbie seemed to consider something for a second, then

she said, "You might as well know, I guess. Don't tell anyone at school, but my name's not really Debbie Cromwell."

"It isn't? What is it then?" Yselle had spent a lot of time thinking up other names for Debbie Cromwell and the rest of the cheerleaders, so she was interested in knowing the answer to this.

"It's Hhh."

"Hhh?"

"Hhh. I'm an assistant fashion engineer from Planet Pentathlon. We produce the hottest clothing lines in this quadrant, did you know that?"

"No," Yselle said.

"We're new around here," explained Walter.

"It's my job to hang around Earth and pick up on the new trends: clothes, hairstyles, accessories, that sort of thing. But not music. Music is not my job."

"So you're an alien?" Yselle was having a hard time with all this. Her nastiest suspicions about Debbie Cromwell were coming true.

"Yes, I'm an alien."

"And you look like us," Walter said. Debbie Cromwell (also known as Hhh from Planet Pentathlon) was the first alien he had seen so far who could walk down the halls of East Weston Northside High and look normal. Relatively normal, at least.

"Not exactly." Debbie pointed to her straight, petite nose. "This is fake. It hides the extra eye."

Walter tried not to look at her nose. If they ever got back to Earth, he would never be able to pay attention in economics class again.

"I'm here on Ice Planet B to meet with my fashion subcommander and drop off my sketches for the new spring designs. I told the school I was visiting colleges. I should be back by Monday. When are you heading back?"

"Our spaceships are in the garage for repairs. Engine trouble," Walter said, bending the truth a little.

Debbie looked out through the bay windows of the lobby. "Speaking of engine trouble, what do you think happened to those two buses?"

In front of the hotel, the Interplanetary Diamond's two antigravity shuttle buses were pulling up to the docking ports. Each had fresh dents and scratches along opposite sides, as if they had been smashing into each other as they drove.

That was, in fact, exactly what had happened. Against their better judgment, the two hotel employees had allowed Uxno and Fip to drive the buses. Walter and Yselle stared at the results of this very bad decision.

"Anyway, it was nice to see you, but I think we'd better be going," Walter said, slipping past Debbie and toward the front doors. Yselle was already halfway there.

Debbie Cromwell (known to her closest friends as Hhh), watched Walter and Yselle run over to the Wotwots and Lirgonians, who were climbing out of their respective buses, spoiling for a fight.

She shook her head. "Freshmen."

17

The next morning, Walter was eating breakfast at the Interplanetary Diamond Hotel's complimentary buffet. Yselle was there, and so were a few crew members from the *Gilded Excelsior* and the WSS *Ferlinghetti*. Despite the fact that Jerry had specifically told them not to, Uxno and Fip had sent most of their crews back to the Spacecraft Repair Plaza. Uxno had sent his crew because he couldn't believe that a big job like pulling the spaceships apart could be done properly without lots of help. Fip had sent his crew because he didn't like the idea of so many Lirgonians so close to the WSS *Ferlinghetti* without someone to keep an eye on them.

Walter returned from the buffet table with more toast and a glass of orange juice. He would have liked some scrambled eggs, but there weren't any. He thought that was kind of odd until he overheard one of the hotel employees saying that the scrambled egg machine was missing. It had been stolen by Space Mice from Galaxy Four.

Walter sat down between Yselle and Voo. "How are the repairs going?" he asked.

"Not well," Voo said, glumly nudging a sausage with her butter knife. "The Channeling Nougat Interference Space Drive is completely out of alignment, and the Gravity Impersonator is running on its backup module."

"Combine the cost of repairs with this exorbitant hotel, and we're going to be miles overbudget," said Uxno, even glummer than Voo. "I don't know how I'm going to fill out the expense report."

"Maybe you should have thought about that before you rammed your flying saucer into us," Fip growled.

"That was a perfectly brilliant piece of space-battle strategy! If you had just done what you were supposed to do and flown over us, everything would have been fine. But you didn't fly over us, you flew into us. And now look where we are."

"Broken down," said Voo.

"Bankrupt," added Snartmer.

"You do realize that we'll probably get demoted for this, don't you?" said Uxno. "We'll end up working as quality control inspectors in a nougat processing center, and it'll be all your fault. It's no wonder that the ungratefulness of the Wotwot people is a byword throughout the galaxy."

Fip's beady little eyes got wide. "Ungrateful! This from the culture that hasn't even invented the thank-you note yet? Man, I ask you! I don't have to take this from the culture that plays kazoos at its weddings! From the culture whose national anthem is light jazz! And it's not as if you're the only ones who are suffering here, buddy!"

"That's right," Burkhardt said. "Our space vessel gets totaled, we have to wire back to Planet Wotwot for more money, and we don't even have a victory to show for it yet. You can bet your little red suits that the Style Council is going to have some unpleasant questions for us, man."

"I've seen your Style Council," snapped Uxno, "and any organization with members as ugly as those should keep its opinions to itself."

"Hey! I've had just about enough of you!"

"What are you going to do about it?"

"When we get our ship back, we're going to throw down on you like nobody's business!" Fip shouted. "Yselle Meridian is going to show your rat-faced little general exactly how space battles are supposed to be fought. We know she's watched more movies than he has!"

"We will finish what we started and start something you will not be able to finish, Wotwot!"

"Wait a second!" Walter held up his hands. He was a little annoyed about the "rat-faced" crack, but he let it go. There was something more important. He had an idea. All morning he had been racking his brain to figure out a way to resolve the feud between the Wotwots and Lirgonians. Since his brain hadn't had any exercise for months, it had been slow going, but now he finally had something.

"Okay, say you both get your spaceships fixed, and we go and start the battle again," Walter said. "What happens then?"

"We win," said Uxno and Fip together.

"I don't know," said Walter. "I mean, Yselle and I are good generals and everything . . ." He tried not to look at Yselle when he said this, because he knew they would both crack up. "But neither one of us can guarantee a victory."

Snartmer patted Walter on the back. "We believe in you."

"So do we," said Burkhardt. "Not you. Her. We believe in her. You know what I mean."

Yselle spoke up. "What I think Walter is trying to say is that if we go back into space and have another big battle, the same thing could happen all over again."

"Embarrassment?" asked Fip.

"Extra expense?" asked Uxno.

"Exactly," said Walter.

Yselle continued. "If your home planets are going to get mad because you had to repair your ships once, just think how they'll feel if you have to do it twice."

"That's not cool," said Fip. "That's not cool at all."

"So what are you saying?" Voo wanted to cut right through to the important matters. She also wanted to get back to the buffet before all the Neptune Danish was gone.

"I'm saying that you can solve your problems without having to fight again."

Uxno stared at Walter in horror, as if he had taken the last of the Proxima Centauri Waffles. "But we can't *not* fight!"

"Yeah, man, fighting's the whole point," Fip agreed.

"We have to have a winner. Somebody's got to win the war."

"Don't worry, there will be a winner." Walter tried to keep both sides calm so they would at least listen to his idea. "We'll have a winner, but nobody has to get shot at. Or blown up. Or run into. Or bankrupted."

Uxno and Fip were silent. Both of them liked the sound of

that, but neither wanted to admit anything. After all, their home planets had sent them out to fight a war, and their supervisors might be upset if they ended up doing something else.

Finally, it was Snartmer who said, "What is it?"

"A race."

"A *what*?" said nearly everyone.

"I like it," announced Yselle. Walter beamed. "A race. That's a really good idea."

"Why?"

"Who thinks it's a good idea?"

"Why a race?"

"How's that better than fighting?"

Those were just some of the responses that the Wotwots and the Lirgonians had to Walter's plan.

Instead of trying to deal with them all individually, Walter just shouted louder. "Now just wait a second! Listen to what I'm trying to say! The reason we're all out here is because the Wotwots want to prove that they're better than the Lirgonians, and the Lirgonians want to prove that they're better than the Wotwots, right?"

"We don't need to prove anything," said Uxno. "Just look at the way we dress."

"The whole universe knows we're better than the Lirgonians," said Fip. "The only people who need it proved are the Lirgonians themselves."

Walter stood up, excited. "See, that's my point! All you want to do is show each other who's best. You don't have to fight a war to do that."

"Now that you mention it, we've been fighting this war for

three hundred years, and it really hasn't gotten us anyplace," said Snartmer.

"That's what's so good about a race." Yselle stood up next to Walter. "This way you know you'll have a winner and a loser, and no one's in any danger."

"That does sound kind of nice," said Burkhardt. He and Snartmer pushed their chairs back from the table and stood up.

At the end of the table, Uxno and Fip sat quietly, frowning.

Walter had another idea. "Uxno, I think this is your best chance to beat the Wotwots. As your general, I advise you to do this."

"Me, too," said Yselle to Fip.

"Will we have time to modify our ships?" Voo asked. "Right now the *Gilded Excelsior* is rigged for maximum destructive capability, not maximum speed."

Walter nodded. "Sure. As much time as you want. Both of you."

Voo stood up as well.

All five of them were standing now, watching Uxno and Fip expectantly.

Uxno glanced quickly at Fip, then up at Walter. "You really advise this course of action?"

"Absolutely."

"Well, if it will save money and hand the Wotwots the red mitten of defeat, I agree to the plan," Uxno said, standing.

"If he's hip to it, so am I." Fip stood up. "Let's race."

18

They ran to the front desk and hurriedly paid the bills. Outside, they charged through the snow, all the way back to Jerry & Mo's Spacecraft Repair Plaza. There was no one in the lobby, so they went on through to the landing field, eager to tell the two spaceship crews what they had decided.

What they found were the mechanics and the two crews, wrapped in parkas and hunched over against the wind, drinking coffee out of little paper cups.

What they did not find were the two spaceships. All that remained where the *Gilded Excelsior* and the WSS *Ferlinghetti* used to stand were two shallow depressions in the ground and a litter of tiny footprints, rapidly filling up with snow.

Jerry noticed the new arrivals and went to meet them. "Space Mice from Galaxy Four," he said, shaking his head slowly.

19

Somewhere else, two space vehicles stood inside a large metal barn. One was a flying saucer with a big dent on its top. The other was a rocket ship with huge tail fins and an ugly rip along one side.

Aboard the flying saucer, better known as the *Gilded Excelsior*, the occupants were very happy. They were also very small. They were three Space Mice from Galaxy Four, and they had just accomplished their mission.

Sitting in a corner of the captain's chair, the leader of this team of Space Mice wiggled his whiskers with pleasure. The transport had been perfect. Things had gone exactly as planned. It had been a good idea to wait until the two ships had been separated. Once the Snow Lizard mechanics had pulled the two ships apart, they took a coffee break, and then the Space Mice had leaped into action. By the time everyone came back from the lobby of the repair plaza, the two ships were gone.

But the Space Mouse team leader knew that their biggest

challenge was still ahead. He gave a squeak, and his two team members joined him on the chair. Together they scrambled up to the top of the headrest. They waited for a second to catch their breath, then the team leader squeaked again and they jumped from the chair toward a spot on the control panel. They missed, sliding off the control panel and bouncing onto the floor.

They tried it again, and missed the spot again. As they raced back into position for another attempt, the team leader wondered whether the Space Mice on the WSS *Ferlinghetti* were having any better luck.

The third time worked. The three mice landed together on a large green button labeled THIS OPENS THE DOOR. The combined weight of their furry little bodies pressed the button down, and the exit door slid open on the other side of the room.

Squeaking with joy, the Space Mice jumped off the control panel and scurried down the exit ramp. They were home.

20

Uxno was upset. **"What am I going to do about this? I'm not** insured for Space Mice."

"Neither are we," said Fip, who didn't sound much happier.

Everyone—Wotwots, Lirgonians, Snow Lizard, humans, and Bookshelf Tribalist—was crowded into the lobby of Jerry & Mo's, trying to keep out of the cold. Jerry, the Snow Lizard mechanic, had struggled through the crowd to hand out coffee to the new arrivals, and he was now standing inconspicuously under a sign that read THE OWNERS OF THIS SERVICE PLAZA ARE NOT RESPONSIBLE FOR ANY DAMAGE OR THEFT OF VEHICLES LEFT ON THE PREMISES. ESPECIALLY IN THE CASE OF SPACE MICE FROM GALAXY FOUR.

"If it's any consolation," Jerry said, "I've never heard of anything this big disappearing before. Maybe we should call the news. You guys could get interviewed on Channel 6.5."

Fip shuddered at the idea. "No way. If word gets back to Planet Wotwot that we lost our spaceship, we'll be complete laughingstocks."

Walter and Yselle were balanced on the back of one of the

couches, with their feet up on the seat. "If the Space Mice took your ships, where did they take them *to*?" Yselle asked.

Walter just shrugged.

"Nobody knows," Burkhardt said. His knitted booties were soggy with snow, and he was standing next to the space heater trying to dry them out.

"You mean that nobody has ever been able to follow them back to where they come from?"

"Never," said Snartmer. He had worked his way over to the coffee machine and was refilling his paper cup.

"Has anybody ever tried?"

"Well . . . No. I don't think so. I mean, if anybody had ever tried and succeeded, we probably would have heard about it, right?"

"So why doesn't anybody try?" said Yselle.

"There's that story about the first mate on one of the long-distance flying-saucer missions. He tried to track down the Space Mice, and he disappeared," Snartmer said.

"I heard that story," said Burkhardt, "but it wasn't a first mate on a flying saucer. It was the owner of a poetry bar on Alpha Centauri Nine. He wanted to see why his cocktail weenies kept disappearing, so he hid back in the storeroom one night. No one ever saw him again."

"Spooky," said Snartmer.

"Spooky," agreed Burkhardt.

Yselle frowned. "So all you have, really, is a story about somebody disappearing that could have happened anywhere, or it might not have happened at all. It sounds to me like no one knows for sure what these Space Mice actually do."

"I don't dig. What are you getting at?" Burkhardt asked.

Yselle pointed out the window. "This: why don't we try to find out where the Space Mice take all the stuff they carry off? It can't just vaporize. They have to do something with it. Maybe we can find out what happened to our ships."

"Sounds good to me," said Walter. He had been trying to get used to the idea of spending the rest of his life on Ice Planet B with the Lirgonians. Now there was suddenly another choice.

Snartmer and Burkhardt were not so sure.

"I don't know. It sounds like a one-way ticket to Vanishville, you know?" said Burkhardt.

"A lot of people think the Space Mice from Galaxy Four are invisible. Maybe nobody can catch them," said Snartmer.

Yselle tried to be patient. "If we don't find the spaceships, what then? You both have to go back to your home planets and tell them what happened, right?"

"The Style Council is not going to be happy to hear that the entire Wotwot space armada is missing. Not happy at all."

"We're still making payments on the *Gilded Excelsior*. They'll probably take that out of our paychecks."

"So would you rather go back home or would you rather try to track down the Space Mice?" Yselle looked at them expectantly.

"When you put it that way, you make a lot of sense," said Snartmer.

"We can't just sit around and do nothing," Walter goaded. "That won't get us anywhere, right? What's the worst thing that could happen?"

"We could disappear without a trace," said Burkhardt. "And

to tell you the truth, that's got to be better than explaining things to the Style Council. Those guys can get awfully square about this stuff when they want to."

Snartmer and Burkhardt left, pushing their way through the crowd in search of the two captains.

A little later they returned with Uxno and Fip. Yselle repeated her idea to them. Neither one really liked it, but they both agreed with Burkhardt and Snartmer that it was better than any other option they had.

The first thing they had to figure out was what to do with the crews of the two spaceships. It was going to be difficult, dangerous work tracking the Space Mice from Galaxy Four, and it would probably be even harder if fifty Lirgonians and Wotwots all went at it at the same time. It was going to be expensive, too, since they would all have to stay in the hotel for however long it took, and nobody had any idea how long that would be.

So Uxno and Fip bought each Lirgonian or Wotwot a second-class ticket home on the Trans-Galactic Express Bus Line and told them to keep their mouths shut. If anyone asked, they were supposed to say that they were sent home as part of a super-secret project to defeat the enemy once and for all. Then they were supposed to change the subject. Uxno and Fip hoped that this story would hold up until they had recaptured the *Gilded Excelsior* and the WSS *Ferlinghetti*.

After seeing the rest of the Lirgonians off from Ice Planet B's main bus terminal, Uxno, Snartmer, Voo, and Walter returned to the repair plaza, which had become their base of operations. Although Jerry and Mo really didn't have to, they wanted to help out all they could. This was the first time the Space Mice from Galaxy Four had stolen anything major from their shop, and they felt bad about it.

Fip, Burkhardt, and Yselle were already back, since the Wotwots had left on an earlier bus. They had set up a card table in the middle of the lobby and spread out a large piece of paper on it. They were drawing elaborate diagrams when the Lirgonians and Walter arrived.

"You're here. Good," Fip said, looking up. "We're trying to build a perfect Space Mouse trap."

Yselle pointed to one of the diagrams. "This is our best idea so far. I'm not sure it's going to work."

Burkhardt was more enthusiastic. "Sure it is. See, we bend back a big spatula, and when the Space Mouse steps on it, he sets off the trigger and it sends him flying into this net over here." He tapped another part of the diagram. "Then we just gather up the net, grab the mouse, and make him tell us where the ships are."

"What about the trigger?" Voo asked. "How does that work?"

"And why would the Space Mouse want to climb onto a bent spatula?" added Snartmer.

Fip frowned at them. "Look, it's just an idea, okay? Can you think of anything better?"

"I think the big problem is not how to catch the Space

Mice but how to make them show up in the first place," Walter said. "Aren't they supposed to be pretty mysterious? Don't they just appear and disappear whenever they feel like it?"

"Exactly," said Uxno.

Yselle put her fingers to her temples, something she did when she was thinking hard. Walter always thought it made her look like she was trying to read someone's mind.

"Do you remember what they did in *The Thing from Another World?*" she asked Walter.

"The 1951 version, the one with James Arness and Douglas Spencer?"

"Yeah. When they wanted to trap the Thing, what did they do? They put out something it wanted, and it came out into the open to get it. We could do the same thing."

Walter snapped his fingers. "What do Space Mice like?"

The aliens looked at each other and shrugged.

"Gee . . . All kinds of things," said Snartmer, finally.

"What were the last few things they took from you guys?" Walter asked the Lirgonians.

"Well, there was the Semi-Transparent Nougat Regulator," said Voo.

"And the official ship's registry of wing-nut technical specifications. And a kazoo," added Snartmer.

"And my copy of *The Globular Galaxy Bagpipe Orchestra's Greatest Hits,*" said Uxno.

"So what does that all sound like?" Walter prompted.

Fip answered. "The products of a diseased mind. Who listens to bagpipe orchestras?"

"Hey!"

"Come on, focus!" Yselle said.

Burkhardt waved a tentacle. "I've got it! I know what it is!"

"What?"

"It's junk! It's all junk! The Space Mice steal junk!"

"Pardon me?" Uxno exclaimed. "Are you describing the *Gilded Excelsior* as *junk*? Is that what I just heard?"

"Hold on," Walter said. "Forget about the spaceships for a second. Aside from those, the Space Mice have always stolen odd things that were lying around, right? Just gadgets and things."

"Tchotchkes. Knickknacks," Fip said. "I get it. You're saying that if we spread around enough interesting stuff, the Space Mice will come to us."

"I think that's the answer," Walter said.

Uxno shrugged. "You may be correct. But how do we put together enough gizmos to make sure the Space Mice visit us?"

"Who in the universe has that much junk?"

21

"Hello?" The voice on the other end of the video telephone sounded sleepy and confused.

Uxno peered at the screen. "Spherical, is that you? I can't see anything on your side."

"Sorry. It's warming up." Even as she spoke, the darkness on the video telephone's screen began to reveal the image of Spherical Mattress Stoyanovich.

"Did we wake you?" Uxno asked.

"Yes." If it was possible for a giant thumb to look annoyed, Spherical Mattress Stoyanovich was looking annoyed.

"Look, we have a favor we need to ask of you." Quickly, Uxno told her about their plan to catch a Space Mouse from Galaxy Four. If they were going to attract a Space Mouse, Uxno said, they were going to need a lot of junk, and no one had more junk than Spherical.

What they wanted was a shipment of Spherical's best gizmos, her most interesting doodads, and her neatest-looking spare parts. And could she bring it over to Ice Planet B as soon as possible, since they wouldn't be able to come to the space station and pick it up?

On Space Station Stoyanovich it was four in the morning, and Spherical Mattress Stoyanovich was not thinking clearly. If she had been wide awake, she would have asked questions such as: "Why do you want to catch Space Mice?" or "How did you ever end up on Ice Planet B?" But she didn't. All she wanted to do was get rid of Uxno as fast as she could, so she said, "Sure."

"Do you mean that?"

"Of course I mean it." Spherical leaned forward to shut off the video telephone.

"And it will arrive soon? We really do need it desperately."

"I'm getting out of bed right now. I'll be there as soon as I can. Jeez," Spherical Mattress Stoyanovich said, and hung up.

Uxno came back out into the lobby. He had been using the video telephone in Jerry and Mo's back office, a room that was much too small to fit everyone.

"She's coming," Uxno said.

"Did she want to know why we needed all this stuff?" asked Fip.

"She didn't ask anything about it."

"Good." Fip, like Uxno, was concerned that if Spherical Mattress Stoyanovich found out about the cooperation between the Lirgonians and the Wotwots, she would surely tell Mong Overthruster, and then they would never hear the end of it.

A couple of hours later, Walter and Yselle were making two-headed snowmen in front of Jerry and Mo's office when they saw a spaceship descend through the heavy clouds. It was very large and shaped like an overturned washtub with metal doors all around the sides. It made a low rumbling sound as it eased down onto the repair plaza's landing field, disappearing from view behind the protective walls.

By the time Walter and Yselle arrived, one of the doors was open and Spherical Mattress Stoyanovich was climbing out. Behind her was one of the palm-tree aliens that Walter had seen back on the space station. The Wotwots and Lirgonians were already there, waiting.

"Lucky for you I've been out collecting and haven't had time to unload the ship yet," Spherical said, making her way down the ladder. "I found some real whizbang quantum converters this time, too. If you're interested, I can let you have them for an unbelievable price. I'd hardly believe it myself."

It was at this moment that Spherical turned around and noticed her audience was not only the three Lirgonians but the Wotwots as well.

"Wait just a minute here," she said, looking from Uxno to Fip and back again. "What are all you guys doing here? Why aren't you off fighting? What the heck is going on?"

Uxno sighed. "Can you keep a secret?" he asked.

"Sure I can."

Behind Spherical, Walter noticed that the palm-tree alien was shaking its fronds.

Uxno must not have seen this, or maybe he just thought the alien was shivering with the cold. Either way, he and Fip told Spherical Mattress Stoyanovich the story about how they had stopped here for repairs and the Space Mice from Galaxy Four had stolen their space vehicles. They tried to keep it short, but with a story as bizarre as this one, it was hard to do.

When they were finished, Spherical quivered with disbelief. "Well, now I've heard everything. And you guys really think you can catch one of those Space Mice with all the junk I've brought with me?"

"That's the plan," said Fip.

"All right, but only on one condition."

"What?"

"That if you catch one of the little guys and get famous, you have to tell everyone that Space Station Stoyanovich is your favorite intergalactic truck stop." Spherical Mattress Stoyanovich didn't have the most popular general-purpose space station in her entire hemiquadrant just because of her good looks. Inside that giant thumb was a great brain for business. If Uxno and Fip did manage to catch a Space Mouse, they could end up as celebrities, and a celebrity endorsement could turn Spherical's truck stop into a tourist attraction. And if Space Station Stoyanovich became a tourist attraction, Spherical would make a ton of cash. It was a sound business risk.

Uxno considered the offer for a second, then agreed.

"All right! Let's unload some junk!"

In no time at all, they had taken everything out of Spherical Mattress Stoyanovich's ship and spread it on the snowy surface of Jerry and Mo's landing field. Everyone was busy. The

Snow Lizards were helping Spherical and the palm-tree alien finish unloading. Voo was arguing with Fip about the best way to arrange everything to attract Space Mice. Snartmer was patching holes in the high wall around the landing field, so that once the Space Mice got in, it would be hard for them to get back out. Uxno paced through the debris, scratching his whiskers. He was trying to decide where the Space Mice would be most likely to go first. Once he knew that, he would be able to put everyone in the best positions for an ambush.

Walter stood at the top of a motorized ladder, hanging Christmas lights and Chinese lanterns. Spherical had gotten these cheap at a going-out-of-business sale in the Crab Nebula, and Walter thought they added a nice touch. From his high viewpoint, Walter could look out over the whole area. From what he had learned about the Space Mice from Galaxy Four, this looked like a place they wouldn't be able to resist. Except for the paths that crisscrossed the landing field, every inch of ground was covered with bits and pieces and useless contraptions from every planet in the universe. It was waist-deep in most places.

The door from the lobby opened, and Yselle and Burkhardt arrived. They were carrying several bulky packages. They had been to the Ice Planet B Super-Mall to pick up some special supplies, and it looked like they had been successful.

Walter drove his motorized ladder over to them. They were still standing in the door, amazed at the transformation that had taken place while they were away.

The motorized ladder rumbled to a halt. "What do you think?" Walter asked.

Yselle craned her neck to look up at Walter. "All this stuff was in Spherical's spaceship? It must be worse than my brother's car in there!"

"I think it's beautiful," Burkhardt said. "It's eclectic. Junk is very chic."

"Then take a look at this." Walter slid down the ladder rail and flipped the switches next to the lobby door. The hundreds of yards of Christmas lights and Chinese lanterns blazed to life.

Burkhardt's tiny eyes got wide. "It's extraordinary."

"It looks like a winter carnival at the East Weston Central Junkyard," Yselle said.

Uxno had finished his tour, and he joined Walter, Yselle, and Burkhardt. "I think we have created something no Space Mouse will be able to resist," he said. "When this is all over, we must congratulate ourselves."

"If it works."

"I am completely confident. Did you find everything at the mall?"

Yselle set down her packages and helped Burkhardt with his. "Yes. We got butterfly nets, one for everyone. They had just enough in stock. The clerk at Butterfly Emporium looked at us kind of funny, but we got them."

Uxno rubbed his mittens together with delight. "Good. No Space Mouse will be able to escape from those. What about the bells?"

"We found those, too. Five bells, each with a different tone. And a ball of string."

"Too cool."

"Tell me again why you wanted those," Burkhardt said.

"In a moment. I'll explain it to everyone at once. But first take these." Uxno handed small yellow walkie-talkies to Yselle and Burkhardt. Walter already had one clipped to his belt.

"These are Short-Range Z-Spectrum Communications Devices," Uxno said. "Spherical bought them near the Brioche Quasar, so you know they're good quality. These will make it easier to stay in touch once things start to move quickly."

Uxno spoke into his walkie-talkie. "Attention, all Space Mouse hunters, attention, all Space Mouse hunters. If you will gather near the door, we will now go over the final details of this glorious and surely not-doomed-to-failure plan. Thank you."

When everyone arrived, Uxno held up the bells and shook them. They made a tinny, jangling sound in the cold air. "Working together with Fip, Spherical, and the Snow Lizards, we have picked the five things that the Space Mice will most likely want to steal. We will tie a bell to each of these. As you can see"—Uxno rang each bell by itself—"the bells all have different tones. That way, when you hear one ringing, you will be able to tell instantly what it is tied to and know exactly where to go."

Uxno then went through each of the five items, from the Automated Flower-Arranging Device to the half-empty box of Plasma Chocolate from the Lesser Blue Galaxy. He tied a bell to each of them and made sure that everyone knew which bell went with which object. He also made sure that everyone knew where on the landing field each object was going to be. As Uxno said, it would have been a tragedy if someone heard the bell for the box of chocolates and ran off in the direction of the Chrome-Plated Fourth-Dimensional Box Wrench Set.

When Uxno was satisfied that everyone, even Voo and the palm-tree alien, knew the system, Fip took over.

"It looks like everything's just about as good as it's going to get," he said. "The Space Mice should show up as soon as they think the coast is clear. It's time to hide. Disappear City."

Quickly, Fip directed where they should hide among the junk, making sure that the Space Mouse hunters were spread out evenly across the landing field.

Walter and Yselle were both stationed on the far side of the field, near a broken-down Interstellar Economy Cruiser that Jerry and Mo's employees were trying to fix.

They reached Walter's spot first. He took the butterfly net in one hand and the walkie-talkie in the other, and wedged himself into a comfortable position between two large piles of junk.

"Call me if anything interesting happens," Yselle said, heading off toward her position.

"You bet." Before Yselle disappeared entirely, Walter called, "This is kind of exciting, isn't it?"

"My mom always says, 'It's only fun until someone gets hurt.' Good luck." Then she was gone.

Walter settled in, tried not to think about the cold, and waited for the Space Mice.

22

Sometime later, three tiny electric blue shapes cruised merrily through the mounds of junk collected from the eight corners of the cosmos.

The Space Mice from Galaxy Four were in heaven. This was, without a doubt, the single neatest place any of them had ever seen. There was so much to look at (and so much to steal) that they quickly split up to cover more ground.

One of the Space Mice darted under a barricade of wrecked spaceship hulls to see what was on the other side. Illuminated by the twinkling lights, the Space Mouse raced from one useless gizmo to the next, finding each object more and more exciting.

Then it stopped. It sat up on its back legs, with its whiskers vibrating and its eyes glazed over in disbelief. Up above it, on top of some old tires, was a Marvelous Thing.

It was the Turbo-Pulsar Industries Breakfast Buddy 6000.

The Breakfast Buddy 6000 was an alarm clock, a toaster, a coffee machine, a bagel slicer, an egg scrambler, and a bacon fryer. It was all that and so much more. It was the perfect combination of robot and kitchen appliance. It had little wheels to roll itself around and provide its owner with breakfast in bed. It had long arms so it could grab the newspaper off the front step and water the plants. It could even discuss the latest sports scores and give you advice about your investments.

The Space Mouse looked at it longingly. The Space Mouse did not care that the Turbo-Pulsar Industries Breakfast Buddy 6000 had been recalled to the factory because of a design flaw. The Space Mouse did not care that if you refused breakfast three days in a row, the Breakfast Buddy 6000 would take offense and wake you up by pouring hot coffee on the plants and throwing bagels at your head.

As far as the Space Mouse was concerned, this was the greatest object in the universe. There was no way the Space Mouse was going to leave without it.

In one try, the Space Mouse leaped from the ground to the top of the machine. It was then that the Space Mouse discovered something strange about this particular Breakfast Buddy 6000. There was a big tin cowbell tied to the Breakfast Buddy's top handle.

23

Walter heard the voice on the walkie-talkie half a second after he heard the sound of the bell.

"It's ringing! It's ringing!" The voice was Snartmer's.

"Go get it!" was Uxno's response.

"Oh, right." Walter immediately heard a thunderous crash from the other end of the landing field. It was Snartmer leaping from his hiding place and knocking over the piled-up junk.

Now Fip was broadcasting. "I see him! He's got the Breakfast Buddy 6000!"

"Attention!" said Uxno. "Close in on the self-propelled breakfast machine! Repeat, the self-propelled breakfast machine! Hurry! We are in danger of losing mouse containment!"

There were more crashes as everyone rushed to obey Uxno's command. Walter jumped to his feet and ran toward the sound of the ringing bell. As he made his way around the maze of junk, he saw something dart through a side passage and off in another direction. At first it looked like the Breakfast Buddy 6000 had gone wild and taken off on its own, but then Walter saw that it wasn't driving, it was being carried. Under the machine, carrying the thing on its back, was a glowing Space Mouse. The cowbell was still tied to the machine, and it rang loudly as the mouse ran.

Walter stood there for a second, openmouthed in surprise, until a large butterfly net swooped down over his head.

"Watch it! What do you think you're doing!" Walter shouted, pushing at the net's handle.

"Sorry." It was Burkhardt. "I thought you were the mouse."

"Do I look like the mouse?"

"I was just swinging at anything that moved. I thought my chances were pretty good."

The walkie-talkie crackled. "It's over here! It's by the sprinkler system!" This voice belonged to Jerry the Snow Lizard.

"Then there must be two of them!" Voo reported. "I'm chasing the one with the Breakfast Buddy, and we're nowhere near the sprinkler!"

"There's one standing right next to me. Hey! I think it's giving me the finger!" said Fip.

"No one panic!" Uxno shouted to the mob of Space Mouse hunters. "Break up into small groups to chase each Space Mouse! This is what you should do . . ." His next words were drowned out by a blast of static interference caused by a low-flying rocket ship with a faulty electrical system. The owners of the rocket had been planning to stop at Jerry & Mo's for repairs, but after getting a look at the lights and the bedlam, they blasted right back into space.

Without Uxno's advice, the bedlam got even worse. They all took off in random directions toward whatever Space

Mouse they thought was closest, swinging their butterfly nets wildly. Snartmer and Fip managed to get their nets over each other and wasted valuable time trying to get free while their Space Mouse escaped. Mo, the Bookshelf Tribalist from the Upper Esophageal Star Cluster, got wedged between two walls of junk as she chased another Space Mouse through a narrow path. Uxno, not looking where he was going, ran right into her and knocked himself silly.

Walter and Burkhardt continued to chase after the mouse with the Breakfast Buddy 6000. They were not doing well. Whenever they thought they were gaining on the little creature, it would make a sharp turn and veer off down another passage, widening the gap again. Walter was amazed that it could run so fast, especially with a robot kitchen appliance on its back. If someone had tied one of those to Walter's back, he wasn't sure if he'd have been able to move at all.

The Space Mouse must have realized that things were getting serious, because at that moment it threw off the burden it had been carrying. As the mouse, now a lot more nimble, raced toward an intersection of paths, the machine bounced to a stop right in Walter's way.

Walter tripped and went flying. As he fell, he threw the butterfly net ahead of him, hoping to trap the Space Mouse by some lucky chance.

The net missed the mouse, but it hit the ground right in front of the creature and made it stop for half a second. In that half second, another butterfly net swung down, trapping it.

Yselle stepped out from one of the crossing paths.

"Gotcha," she said.

24

They were all gathered around a small card table in Jerry
and Mo's back room. Overhead, a single lightbulb burned. On
the table was a Tupperware box.

Inside the box was a Space Mouse from Galaxy Four. It
paced back and forth in its little plastic prison cell, its blue fur
bristling with annoyance.

Fip leaned over the box and scowled. "All right, mouse,
talk!"

"Squeak!" said the Space Mouse.

"That's not good enough. We know you can talk," Fip said.

"Squeak! Squeak!"

"That doesn't fool us. Don't make us use the Device on
you!" said Voo.

Voo had no idea what a Device was, but it sounded sinister
and she thought it might frighten the Space Mouse into talking. After a few seconds of staring at Voo, the Space Mouse
must have figured out that she was bluffing, because it
thrashed its tail and turned toward Fip again.

"What do you have to say about this?" Fip held up a tiny object so the Space Mouse could see it. It was the miniature backpack that the Space Mouse had been wearing when they captured it.

"We have two of these, mouse. One we got from you, and one Snartmer managed to grab from your little furry buddy before he got away. Now, are you going to tell us what these are, or are we going to have to get ugly with you?"

"The spaceships, mouse! Where are the spaceships!" Uxno shouted.

"Squeak!" the Space Mouse said defiantly. It had a feeling that these guys were not as dangerous as they tried to sound.

"Tell us!"

"Squeak! Squeak!"

"I don't think this is working," Yselle said. "Here, let me try something."

"What?" the rest of them asked.

Yselle reached into her jacket pocket and took out a small package. "This is something else I got at the mall."

She started to unwrap it. Across the side of the package, in blue letters, was stamped PROTONIC DAIRY TRIPLE-SHARP ATOMIC CHEDDAR. As she unwrapped the package, an over-powering aroma filled the room.

Yselle broke off a piece of cheese and held it over the box. "Does that smell good?" she asked the Space Mouse.

The Space Mouse's eyes started to water, and its little paws twitched excitedly.

"I bet you're hungry, aren't you?" She held the cheese a little higher. "Would you like some?"

"Squeak!"

"I'm sorry, I can't understand you," Yselle said sympathetically.

"Squeak!"

"I guess you don't want any." She sighed. "That's okay—we'll just eat all this cheese ourselves."

"Not me. I'm allergic to cheese!" said Snartmer.

Walter told him to shut up. He had an idea of what Yselle was trying to do.

"Squeak!"

"What?" Yselle asked, waving the cheese back and forth.

The Space Mouse stared at the cheese. This wasn't fair. It had been prepared for the yelling and the threats, but not this.

There was a long moment when no one said anything.

"All right," the Space Mouse said finally. "I'm talking. Does that make you happy?"

Yselle tossed part of the cheese to the Space Mouse. "Thank you. If you help us out, you can have the rest of this."

"What's your name?" Walter asked.

"I'm B79 Batch 120, Blue Team 19 Gamma," the Space Mouse said, rapidly finishing his piece of cheese, "but my friends call me Barry."

"Hello, Barry," said everyone.

"And before you ask, those backpacks are our Local Matter Removal and Repositioning Systems. That's what lets us take things and disappear with them. See that dial on the side?"

Uxno squinted at the little backpack. "It's a pretty tiny dial."

"We're pretty tiny creatures, genius. Anyway, that dial controls how big a Matter Transportation Hole to make. You press the Activate button and the hole appears. Then you just push whatever you want to take through the hole. That's how we got your spaceships."

"Where are they now? Where did you take them?" Uxno leaned down close to where Barry was sitting. This was the important part.

"We took them home. Honestly, you're not very bright, are you?"

Uxno pretended not to be annoyed. "Home? Where's home?"

"Home is where the cheese is," Barry said, polishing off the last crumbs of what Yselle had given him. "Although this cheese is better, I have to admit."

"What planet, mouse? Where are you from?"

The Space Mouse paused for a second, trying to think. "You know, I'm not really sure. When you have a cool thing like the Local Matter Removal and Repositioning System, it's hard to remember exactly what planet you're on all the time."

"All right, Barry," Fip said, "this is the sixty-four-trillion-dollar question. The whole universe wants to know the answer. Why do you take all this stuff? What do you do with it?"

"We don't do anything with it. It's all for The Boss. That's what The Boss wants."

"*Who is The Boss?*"

"How should I know? I'm just on Blue Team, and Blue Team 19 at that. It's not like I see The Boss every day. I mean, you can't possibly think that I'm all 'Hey, it's The Boss! How ya been, big guy? Wanna split some daiquiris?' Come on! If you guys want information about The Boss, you're tormenting the wrong mouse."

"He's probably right," Voo said.

"The little weasel," added Snartmer.

"Watch it, pajama boy. Listen, guys, if you want to talk to The Boss, go see him yourselves. Use the Local Matter Removal and Repositioning Systems. You've got two of them."

"We may just do that," said Fip, picking up the two tiny backpacks. "Thanks, mouse."

"Yeah, whatever. It doesn't matter to me. This couldn't get any worse. I'm lucky if I don't get demoted down to Paisley Team because of this. Maybe even Burnt Umber Team. Now how about the rest of that cheese?"

25

The wind had picked up out on the landing field. Two groups were huddled together against the cold. In front of them, hovering a foot off the ground, were two swirling disks of electric blue light. The disks threw a strange glow on the features of those who stood nearby, making their faces seem pale and unnatural.

Of course, most of their faces would have looked pale and unnatural anyway, since they were all scared out of their minds. Uxno, Voo, Burkhardt, and Yselle Meridian were scared. Fip, Walter Nutria, and Snartmer were scared. In the office, peering at the scene over the back of the couch, Jerry, Mo, Spherical Mattress Stoyanovich, and the palm-tree alien were scared, too. Since they weren't the ones about to leap through a dimensional portal to face the dangers of a mysterious unknown planet, they were a little less scared, but they were still concerned.

Hiding under the wreck of a 1958 Plymouth Fury with his brick of cheese, Barry the Space Mouse was not scared at all.

He was enjoying himself. When the fun was over, he planned to hitch a ride back home with the next Space Mouse who happened to come along.

In front of the Matter Transportation Holes, it was time to go.

"Are we ready?" Uxno asked.

Everyone nodded, except for the two Wotwots. They had no necks. Instead, they bobbed up and down.

"Snartmer, count us off."

"One for the money," said Snartmer.

Everyone got into place.

"Two for the show," said Snartmer.

Everyone rocked back and forth, ready to jump.

"Three to get ready," said Snartmer.

They all took a deep breath.

"Four to go!"

All together, they leaped into the blue disks and disappeared. There was a slight buzzing sound, then the glowing circles blinked out of existence.

Everyone was gone.

On the landing field, there was no noise but the wind and the soft sound of a mouse chuckling.

26

The first thing Yselle noticed was the smell of electricity.
It smelled just like the time she and Walter had watched
Creature from the Black Lagoon five times in a row and the
VCR had blown up.

The second thing Yselle noticed was that Voo was lying on
her foot.

"Excuse me," she said, prodding Voo with her other foot.
Voo mumbled something and tried to get up. Voo wasn't very
successful, since Burkhardt was sprawled on top of her. The
Wotwot was on his back, flailing his tentacles in an effort to
flip himself right-side-up again. The effort caused him to rock
back and forth, mostly over Voo's stomach.

"Oof" was all that Voo was able to say.

Yselle managed to pull her foot free without kicking Voo
too hard. With the help of Uxno, who had crawled out from
under the pile, they pushed Burkhardt back onto his feet
(such as they were).

"Like, thanks," Burkhardt said, straightening his knitted

wool booties. He looked at the rest of them. "What the heck happened?"

Yselle leaned against a wall. "I feel like I just got off the Whiplash Mountain ride at Velocity World."

"As do I," said Uxno. "I suspect it's a result of the Local Matter Removal and Repositioning System. It must affect our metabolism in strange and exotic ways."

"Ugh. This bites. How do the Space Mice stand it?" Voo had her mittens pressed tightly over her eyes. She knew that if she looked, the room would start to spin again.

"Maybe they're used to it," Yselle said.

"Forget the Space Mice, man, where's Fip?" asked Burkhardt. "And the Earth guy? And that other Lirgonian, what's his name?"

"Snartmer."

"Snartmer, yeah. Where's he?"

"For that matter, where are we?"

As their nausea began to go away, the four of them started to take an interest in their surroundings. They were standing inside a long building that seemed to be a combination warehouse and museum. Junk was everywhere, but it was not messy piles of junk like they had just left behind on Jerry and Mo's landing field. This was orderly junk. As far as they could see in either direction, there was nothing but shelves and boxes and cabinets and display cases, all holding junk. The bigger pieces sat by themselves, arranged in a tidy row along one wall.

"This is crazy. Take a look at this." Burkhardt had opened one of the glass-fronted cabinets and was examining the contents. "This stuff all has labels." He pointed to the tiny white stickers that were on the sides of every single piece.

Voo picked up something that looked like an adjustable oboe and examined it. On its label was written a long string of letters and numbers.

"That's an identification sticker," Voo said. "Somebody's keeping track of all this junk. Who would go to this much trouble?"

Yselle reached over Voo's shoulder and grabbed something off the shelf. "Hey! Those are my dad's." She held up a ring full of keys, which also held a brass disk with I ♥ THE CARDIOVASCULAR SYSTEM engraved on it. (Yselle's dad was a doctor.)

"He lost these months ago." Yselle put the keys in the inside pocket of her coat. "He'll be thrilled that I found them again. Maybe he'll overlook the fact that I snuck out to another planet on a school night."

"Shh!" Burkhardt held up a tentacle. "Did you hear that?"

"What?" Uxno asked. "I heard the jingle of keys. Is that what you meant? I think we all heard that, didn't we?"

"Listen! There it goes again."

"I don't hear anything."

"It's getting closer." Although the Wotwots have no visible ears, they have very sharp hearing.

In time, everybody else heard what Burkhardt was talking about. It was a metallic thumping noise that echoed through the long hallway. It was still a long way off, but it was getting nearer as they listened.

They jumped behind one of the bulky objects that stood

near the wall. It was actually a small pipe organ that had disappeared from a temple of the High Priesthood of Linoleum on Planet Kvit two years ago. It was just big enough to hide all four of them from whatever was coming.

As the noise got closer, they realized that it was footsteps, like someone stomping around in oversize metal galoshes. The sound grew closer still. Finally, it stopped right in front of their hiding place.

After nothing happened for a few seconds, Yselle leaned carefully around the side of the pipe organ to see what was going on.

A giant robot stood in the middle of the hall, not two feet away from her.

Fortunately, it was turned toward the cabinet. It had opened the doors and seemed to be looking for something.

"What's going on?" Uxno whispered.

"Shh!" Yselle was studying the robot. It had a big, streamlined body with flexible metal tubes for arms and legs, and heavy-looking hands and feet. It would have been a frightening sight if its head weren't so small in comparison to the rest of it. From what she could see, the robot's head was just a tiny dome on top of its huge shoulders. It was almost comical, but not quite.

The robot continued to search in the cabinet. It methodically examined each item on each shelf, working its way down to the bottom.

"What's happening?"

"Shh!"

When the robot finished checking the last shelf, it started

to turn around. As soon as she saw it move, Yselle darted back under cover. She waited, trying not to breathe and hoping that the robot hadn't seen her.

In fact, the robot had not seen Yselle. It had, however, noticed a number of footprints in the dust on the floor. Those prints wandered around for a while, stopped in front of the cabinet, then trailed off behind the pipe organ. The robot took a step forward. Its metal legs lengthened until it was tall enough to see what was behind the organ.

With no place to run, Yselle, Uxno, Voo, and Burkhardt stared up in terror as the robot leaned over them.

"May I help you?" the robot asked.

27

Meanwhile, somewhere else, the other group had arrived.
Instead of landing in a jumbled, nauseated heap, they arrived
standing up and feeling fine. They also arrived three feet
above the floor. For half an instant they seemed to hover
there. Then they fell and landed in a jumbled heap. But at
least they weren't nauseated.

"Ow," Snartmer said, standing up and massaging his in-
jured backside. "That hurt a lot."

Walter counted heads and came up with three. "Where is
everybody else?"

"They're probably around somewhere," Fip said. "I'll bet
the Space Mouse didn't tell us how to set those matter trans-
porter things right. 'Turn the dial and press the button'
my little pink tentacles," he scoffed. "I knew there was a
catch."

"Speaking of Space Mice, look around," Walter said.

The room was a maze of plastic tubes. They ran up the
walls, across the ceiling, and through the air. Dozens of plastic

cages were connected to the tubes at various points through-out the room. The multicolored tubes were translucent, and masses of Space Mice from Galaxy Four could be seen racing through them in all directions.

Fip carefully sniffed the air. "What is that smell?"

"I know—it's cedar," Walter said. "I used to have a guinea pig, and that's what I lined the bottom of his cage with. Cedar chips."

"Hey, over here!" Snartmer was kneeling down by one of the cages. Inside, they could see Space Mice leaping out of the tubes that connected to the box, squeaking at other Space Mice, then leaping into other tubes as fast as they could go.

It's a shame that none of them knew how to speak Space Mouse, because they might have learned some very interest-ing things.

Walter stood up. "Look at all these Space Mice. Does this mean that we're in Galaxy Four?" On the other side of the room, a window showed an expanse of starry sky. "Do those stars look right for Galaxy Four?" Walter asked.

Snartmer shook his head. "Walter, there are a billion billion galaxies, and each galaxy has a billion billion stars, and most stars have at least a couple of planets, and a lot of those planets have guys living on them. Without a map, it would take our best computer hours and hours to look at those stars and figure out where—"

"We're in Galaxy Four," Fip said, looking out the window.

"What? How do you know?"

"I can see the front of the building." Fip pointed to a large sign that read WINNER OF THIS YEAR'S GALAXY FOUR CIVIC IMPROVEMENT PRIZE.

"Oh," Snartmer said. "Well, if you want to do it that way, I guess that works, too."

"Has either of you ever been to this galaxy before?" asked Walter.

Snartmer shook his head. "Not me. There isn't a whole lot going on in Galaxy Four. Everybody says so."

"It's a good college galaxy, though," said Fip. "I graduated from the University of Galaxy Four."

"And just what are you three doing here?" The voice from across the room made them all jump. Even the Space Mice were startled for a second.

"You can't be in here!" It was a robot: shiny, a little taller than Walter, and built to look sort of like a hospital nurse. She pointed to a sign on the door that read REALLY AUTHORIZED PERSONNEL ONLY.

"You can't be in here!" she repeated. "You'll disturb the Space Mice! This is a very sensitive procedure!"

"Why?" asked Fip.

The robot reminded Walter of a person he knew. If anyone was ever going to make a robot that looked and acted just like Mrs. Gdansk, his algebra teacher from last year, it would be just like the robot that was talking to them now.

"They're training." The robot sounded exasperated, as if this was the most obvious thing in the world. She led them over to one of the boxes. "You see there, when a Space Mouse gets to that habitat box, one of the Space Mouse Trainers asks it whether it would rather steal a first-edition Herman Melville novel or a Pac-Man video game. If it picks the game, it goes into the green tube. If it picks the book, it goes into the red tube. Each tube leads to a different box with a different question. In the end, the Space Mice get a lot of exercise, and they all end up in habitat boxes with other Space Mice who like to steal the same things."

Snartmer was looking at the tubes, and he saw that many of them ran up through the ceiling or through the walls. "How far do these go?"

"This annex of the Space Mouse Training Center is approximately fifteen miles long."

Snartmer goggled at her. "Fifteen miles!"

"It takes a lot of space to make a proper Space Mouse. And you're disturbing them. Out you go." She started to push them, gently but with determination, toward the doors.

"Wait!" Fip slipped out of her grasp. "Why do you want Space Mouse teams in the first place? Like, what's the point? Somebody spent a pile of cash on this place, but for what?"

"Why do we train Space Mice?" The nurse robot sounded shocked. Not only were these three trespassers, but they were clearly brain-damaged ones. "Because training Space Mice is the Thing to Do."

"The Thing to Do?"

"The Thing to Do." She continued to herd them toward the exit.

By the time they were out in the corridor, Walter remembered a name that Barry the Space Mouse had used. "What about The Boss? Is all this for The Boss?"

The nurse robot frowned at him. "I would never use such a

common, familiar phrase to describe him. You are referring to our Chief Executive Officer. He is the owner and president of our company."

"Now we're getting somewhere," Fip said. "What exactly does this company thing do?"

"Good heavens, I couldn't begin to give you an accurate picture of what our company does. I'm only an assistant supervisor for the Space Mouse Training Facility Annex."

"Then who *could* tell us?"

She looked carefully at the three of them, trying to decide whether to speak or not. Eventually she said, "Well, you could go to the Central Chamber. We don't receive a lot of visitors here, and it's possible that the Chief Executive Officer might take a few minutes out of his busy schedule to explain things to you."

"Really?"

"If you're lucky."

The robot nurse gave them directions and watched Walter, Fip, and Snartmer jog down the hall. She had a feeling that they would not be lucky.

28

It could be worse, Yselle thought. And she was right. The giant robot could have picked them all up and carried them instead of letting them walk. Or it could have just stomped on them with its huge feet as soon as it found them. The way things were, they still had a chance.

She and Uxno were marching down the long warehouse hall. Behind them were Burkhardt and Voo. Behind *them* was the robot, clanking along and making sure they didn't get out of line.

"I demand to know where you are taking us!" Uxno said. It sounded more like a whine than a demand. They had already asked this question, but the robot still hadn't given them an answer.

"As I told you, and your friend, and your lumpy friend, and your other friend with the strange haircut, the first place we are going is *out* of the Storage Complex." The robot had a British accent, which made it seem a little less scary. It was still a giant robot, though, and everyone was careful not to do anything dumb.

"What happens then?" This was the part they wanted to know.

The robot sighed. It sounded like steam escaping from a rusty radiator. "Oh, all right. If it's the only way to make you be quiet, I'll tell you."

"Well?"

"I have no idea what is going to happen. This is a very unique situation. In all my years of service, we have never had to deal with intruders in the Storage Complex before." When it spoke, the multicolored lights on its tiny head flashed. "To say nothing of intruders that have actually stolen something."

"We didn't steal anything!"

"Yes, you did. One of you, and you know who you are, took object number 83a12g057xqf.34. It was supposed to be in the cabinet, and it wasn't. Therefore, I can only conclude—"

"Those were my dad's keys," Yselle said, indignant. "He needs those."

"Now, this is exactly why I'm taking you to the Main Cataloguing Station, young lady."

Yselle scowled at the robot from over her shoulder. She hated being called "young lady" by anyone.

The robot continued. "I will be frightfully honest with you and say that I'm rather out of my depth with this business. I'm a retrieval specialist, you see. When a request for an item comes into the Main Cataloguing Station, it is my job to retrieve it from the Storage Complex. Which is what I was doing when I found you."

Burkhardt was walking backward, facing the robot as it talked. "So that's your entire job? You go and get things?"

"It's slightly more complicated than that," the robot replied, sounding offended, "but I won't bore you with the details. I used to be a placement specialist, but I decided that a change would do me good. And it has."

Uxno stopped suddenly, nearly causing Voo to trip over him. "You haven't seen a large flying saucer lately, have you?" the Lirgonian captain asked.

"No, I haven't. And keep walking, please."

"Are you sure? It's round, it flies, it's probably got a big dent in it?"

"No."

They walked in silence for a few minutes, until Yselle thought of another question: "How much farther is it?"

"It shouldn't be long now. Not much more than a kilometer."

"What?"

"You should feel fortunate that I found you so close to the entrance."

Sometime later, with sore feet and rising nervousness, they arrived at the Main Cataloguing Station. It was a large room with dozens of doors leading off in several directions. The doors were of different sizes, from closet doors to doors big enough for an airplane hangar. A huge open archway led off down another passage.

"This is where it all begins," the robot said. "New material arrives here, where it receives a catalogue number. Then one of the placement specialists puts it in an appropriate section of the Storage Complex."

As he spoke, they saw a Space Mouse race in through the archway with a large box on its back.

"Ah, there's one of our operatives now," the robot said. "They come here from the Arrival Zones with whatever they've carried off, and present it to the facility manager for cataloguing."

On the other side of the Main Cataloguing Station, the Space Mouse dropped its box in front of a beat-up wooden desk and sped away.

"Now that we're here, I'm going to refer you to the care of the facility manager." The giant robot ushered them toward the desk, and they saw another robot sitting behind it. This one was smaller, but it seemed to be of a similar design.

"Terence!" the smaller robot said, "this is most interesting. Whom have you with you?"

"Mr. Chang, these are the intruders. Intruders, this is Mr. Chang."

As Terence the giant robot told the story of how he had discovered the intruders, the lights on Mr. Chang's head glowed with thought. When the story was finished, Mr. Chang said, "Hmm . . . You behaved correctly when you brought them here, but I'm afraid it's more than my job is worth to decide what's to be done with these stealthy prowlers. Would you be so good as to take a moment and guide them to the Chief Executive Officer's Central Chamber? Perhaps he could shed some light on this little affair."

"Chief Executive Officer? Is that who the Space Mice call The Boss?" asked Yselle.

"My dear, I have no idea what the operatives call anything,

although that certainly sounds like something they'd think of as clever."

Terence pointed to the archway with his huge hand. "This way, please."

After another long walk down endless corridors and hallways, Terence stopped them in front of a large, sinister-looking door.

"This is the Central Chamber. I urge you to be on your best behavior," he said. "The Chief Executive Officer is a very busy man, and he has little tolerance for foolishness."

"Then we're in trouble already," Yselle mumbled under her breath.

Terence's lights flashed. "I heard that. And stand up straight. Whoever your instructor at finishing school was, she should be sorely reprimanded."

Terence leaned forward to open the door, and he didn't see the face that Yselle made at him.

Uxno, Voo, Burkhardt, and Yselle crowded into the Central Chamber, followed by the giant robot.

They looked around in amazement. "It's incredible," Yselle said.

29

"It's incredible," Walter said.

He, Fip, and Snartmer were standing in the doorway to the Central Chamber, too amazed to move. It was an unbelievable room. To start with, it was huge, as big as a cathedral, or at least a lot bigger than St. Stanislaus's Church in East Weston, which was the only one Walter was really familiar with. Inside, the room looked like a combination of a rocket ship from an old pulp magazine and a radio set from the 1930s. Scattered all over were enormous science-lab machines, all of them buzzing or hissing or throwing off sparks.

Walter, who had watched Fritz Lang's *Metropolis* by himself one afternoon when Yselle was sick, recognized the place. It was as if he had stepped right into the movie itself. Except that this was in color. And it was on another planet. And Yselle Meridian was waving at him from the other side of the room. Yselle, Voo, Burkhardt, and Uxno.

Actually, Yselle, Voo, Burkhardt, Uxno, and a giant robot.

As the two groups met each other in the middle of the room, Walter, Fip, and Snartmer kept a nervous eye on the giant robot. They couldn't tell whether it had captured their friends or was just a guide.

"Well, I'm glad to see that the Storage Complex was not the only area invaded today," Terence remarked. "I take it you all know each other?"

There was a round of introductions and a lot of general hugging and hand-shaking and being glad that nothing bad had happened to anyone.

Terence waited politely until everyone was finished. "If that's done, I should give you a proper tour of the Central Chamber. This is, as the name suggests, the focal point of our entire—"

"THAT WILL DO, TERENCE!" A rumbling, basso profundo voice echoed through the Central Chamber, nearly knocking everyone off their feet (or tentacles).

"DON'T YOU HAVE ANY DUTIES TO PERFORM?" it boomed.

"Yes, sir," Terence said nervously. "That is an excellent point. I will get right back—"

"GO!"

As quickly and quietly as he could, Terence clanked away toward the Storage Complex.

"Give us back our spaceships!" Uxno shouted into the air. He was guessing that whoever was behind the voice was the chief of this entire operation.

"NO!"

"Who are you?" yelled Fip.

"PREPARE YOURSELVES FOR THE TERROR OF MY GLORY!"

Walter rolled his eyes. So far, he had seen chubby middle-aged guys in footie pajamas, talking thumbs, beatnik rutabagas, furry lizards, and robot nurses. What else could there be?

"LOOK UPON ME, YE MIGHTY, AND DESPAIR!"

They all looked about wildly, trying to see where this fearsome presence would materialize.

"OVER HERE! BY THE THRONE!"

At the end of the room was a raised platform, and on it was a giant high-tech throne made of chrome and green neon with black velvet upholstery. When the group got closer, they saw a person standing in front of it. He wore thick, round glasses and a pointed black beard. Unlike the Beat beards that Fip and Burkhardt wore, this was an evil beard. It was obvious to anyone that whoever could wear a beard like that would have no problem doing evil deeds. His shiny bald head gleamed in the light. He wore a white lab coat over his black turtleneck sweater and slacks. His arms were folded, and he smirked triumphantly at the visitors. "Recognize me now?" he asked, putting down his microphone.

Voo made a strangled noise. "It's . . . It's . . ."

Uxno completed the thought: "It's Doctor X!"

"Wait!" Fip shouted. "I know that guy! When I was at the University of Galaxy Four, he taught my seminar on medium-speed physics and its effect on jazz drumming. But he wasn't a professor. He was just a teaching assistant . . ."

"You mean?"

"Yes!"

"He's . . ."

"Doctoral Candidate X!"

Doctoral Candidate X looked a little less frightening after this. "My thesis is written, okay?" he said. "I'm just revising it before I take it to the review committee."

Fip shrugged. "Whatever you say."

"But it doesn't matter! All of you will tremble with fear when my master plan for ruling the universe is complete! And it's just about to happen! You wait!"

"Oh yeah?" said Voo, who was being brave.

"Yeah."

"So if you're behind the Space Mice and you get everything they steal, what do you do with it all?" Walter said. They had been asking this question of everyone they met, it seemed. Now, finally, someone might give them an answer.

Doctoral Candidate X paced back and forth on his throne platform. "I'm glad you asked that! A truly diabolical plan for intergalactic conquest, such as mine, is too good to keep quiet."

He began to lecture. "As we all know, the real difficulty in becoming ruler of the universe is the expense involved. Take that, for instance." He pointed to a colossal ray gun standing alone and neglected in the corner. "That is my Nucleonic Vector Conquest Ray. Very destructive. Very frightening. But it requires an Illudium Q36 Explosive Space Modulator to function properly. And I don't have to tell you how expensive one of those is."

They all agreed, except for Walter and Yselle, who were having a hard time accepting that this was really happening.

"Especially on a teaching assistant's salary," Doctoral Candidate X said. "And if the dealers find out that you're bent on universal domination, they jack up the price, just like that!" He snapped his fingers. "It's criminal. But then I had my great idea: the universe is filled with all kinds of old junk, and no one notices if little bits of it disappear every once in a while. So I trained my Space Mice, and I built my robots, and I put my plan into motion. Now my work is nearly complete! I have amassed the largest collection of junk ever imagined."

"But *why?*" everyone asked.

" 'But why?' 'But why?' " he mocked. "I'll show you 'but why?'!" He stabbed at a button on his throne's control panel. Behind him a section of the wall slid back to reveal a giant viewscreen.

"Behold! The Terror Fleet of Doctoral Candidate X!"

30

The screen showed a view of space, with hundreds and hundreds of spaceships orbiting around Doctoral Candidate X's planet. Each ship seemed to be made from random bits and pieces, all welded together.

"You're a madman!" Uxno shouted.

"You'll never get away with it!" Fip shouted.

"Those are really ugly spaceships," Burkhardt said.

"They won't fly. They'll fall apart," Voo said.

"Can I use that microphone?" asked Snartmer.

"Fools! It's too late!" Doctoral Candidate X laughed. "There is nothing you can do! You have arrived at the very moment of my triumph! The final Planetary Transponders have just been installed! My Terror Fleet stands ready to depart! No one can stop me now!"

"The *Gilded Excelsior* carried a Planetary Transponder," Voo said.

"So did the *Ferlinghetti*," said Burkhardt. "Hey, give those back!"

"Ha!" Doctoral Candidate X pressed another button, and part of the ceiling rolled away, revealing the night sky above. From out of the floor, a rocket pod emerged, its nose pointed upward, its engines trailing smoke.

"And now it is time to complete the final phase of my fiendish plan! At the head of my fleet, I, Doctoral Candidate X, will invade the Earth!"

"*What?!*" Walter and Yselle shouted.

"You heard me!" Doctoral Candidate X removed his glasses and replaced them with a pair of thickly tinted welders' shades.

"Why the Earth? What has the Earth ever done to you?" Yselle asked.

"Foolish, ignorant children! Foolish, ignorant, unfashionably dressed, unattractive children! Haven't you figured it out by now? Don't you understand?"

"Well, if we did, we wouldn't be asking you," said Walter.

Doctoral Candidate X spread his arms wide. "Can't you see? The Earth is the seat of all coolness in the universe! It's the Grand Central Station of hip!" He spoke to the Wotwots and the Lirgonians: "If you're looking for something cool, where do you go?"

"Earth," they answered automatically.

"And why?"

"Where else would you go?" Snartmer said. "They invented Buddy Holly and pro wrestling and mu shu pork and stuff. I mean, that all doesn't happen by accident, does it?"

"Exactly! Now listen closely—if you ruled the universe, how cool would that be? Pretty darn cool, I assure you. So where would you go to learn how to rule the universe? Keep in mind that ruling the universe is cool."

Yselle and Walter both turned pale.

"Aha! You understand me now," Doctoral Candidate X said. "I would *so* have made a good professor!"

Uxno trembled with the horror of it all. "You monster! What a devilishly cunning plan! You're going to ransack Earth because you think you'll find something that will show you how to conquer the universe!"

"I don't think, I know. I already know exactly what I'm looking for. *Roger Rocket and the Pirates from Ganymede*, part of the Roger Rocket, Space Hero series, published in 1953 by the Adventuretime Publishing Company of Cleveland, Ohio."

"You're wrong, lunatic!" Fip pointed three tentacles accusingly. "I have the entire Roger Rocket series, and that isn't one of them!"

Doctoral Candidate X laughed and pressed another button on his throne's control panel. "It was a limited pressrun, you potato-shaped simpleton! The book was quickly pulled off the market when it was discovered that it contained a complete plan for dominating the cosmos in Five Easy Steps. *Roger Rocket and the Pirates from Ganymede* is one of the most famous lost books in Earth's history, just like Aristotle's *Treatise on Comedy* and Shakespeare's *Hamlet II—The Revenge of Horatio*."

"It will never work!"

"I don't believe you. Besides, what can possibly go wrong? I am completely prepared! I have my Terror Fleet, I have my Space Mice, but I think I'll leave my robots with you."

At that moment the two side doors opened. Terence and the robot nurse entered the room and joined Doctoral Candidate X.

"I hate to rush off like this," he said, jumping from the platform and throwing open the door of the rocket pod, "but you won't be around to take offense much longer."

He turned his attention back to the robots. "Terence! Nurse Ratchet! Give them the Treatment!"

Doctoral Candidate X climbed into the rocket pod's single seat and slammed the door shut behind him. He waved mockingly through the porthole, and the rocket pod took off in a shower of sparks and flame.

When Yselle, Walter, and the rest could see again, the first things they noticed were Terence and Nurse Ratchet, advancing slowly through the smoke.

"Come with us, please," said Terence.

31

They were marching once again through Doctoral Candidate
X's fortress, on their way to a date with the Treatment. "You
do understand that resistance is useless, don't you?" asked
Terence hopefully.

"We'd gathered that, yeah," snarled Yselle.

"Good. It goes so much easier that way."

As they walked, Yselle whispered to Walter, "We've got to
get out of here!"

"I know," he whispered back, "but how?"

"I'm thinking. You think, too. One of us is bound to come
up with something."

Walter wasn't too sure he liked their chances, but he tried
to think anyway. He and Yselle might be the only ones working on an escape; everyone else seemed to be too frightened
of the Treatment.

"What exactly is this Treatment?" Snartmer asked Nurse
Ratchet, who was making sure that her side of the group kept
walking. Snartmer suspected that, whatever the Treatment
was, it wasn't going to be fun.

"The Treatment? Well, young Lirgonian, I don't really know."

"You don't?"

"All I know is that the Chief Executive Officer gives the Treatment to people who annoy him in some way."

"And now, sadly, all of you have become a part of that category," added Terence. "Along with his parents, his former students, and the people who used to own this castle."

"But what does it *do*?" The uncertainty was worse than if the robots had just explained all the gruesome details.

"You'll soon find out," said Nurse Ratchet. "Here we are."

In the center of the Treatment room stood a machine. It was certainly big and scary. It was covered with dials and knobs, and there was a hopper labeled LOAD on the top. On one side a faucet stuck out, with its nozzle over a small, empty jar. Around the room stood shelves with similar jars on them. Except that those jars were all full of a dark liquid. The lumpy goo in the jars reminded Walter of his grandmother Nutria's pickled-egg stew, but here the lumps were moving. As he watched, the goo twisted around and formed faces filled with horror and desperation. He saw one of the faces mouth the words "Help me."

Walter had a feeling he knew what the machine did.

Time was running out. There was a poster on the wall that said "THE UNPLEASANT MACHINE—QUICK REFERENCE." Terence leaned down and began to read it. Walter was getting worried. He was trying to think of a movie where the heroes had escaped from something like this, but his mind drew a blank. He kept staring at the machine. It lurked there in the middle of the room, with a thick power cord trailing off behind it like a tail. Terence stood up.

Walter's eyes got wide. But he wasn't afraid anymore. He knew what to do. "Hey!" he whispered to Yselle, "I need a distraction. Can you make them look over there for a second?" He pointed to the opposite side of the room.

"I can try," she whispered back. Then, all of a sudden, she cried, "Look at that! It's a Space Mouse!"

"So what? They're all over the place. They're impossible to control," said Nurse Ratchet.

"But look! Look!" Yselle pointed furiously. "This one's orange!"

While everyone, including Terence and Nurse Ratchet, hurried over to try to find the orange Space Mouse, Walter went around to the other side of the machine and yanked its power cord out of the wall socket. He kicked the plug out of sight behind a table and got back just as they were deciding that Yselle had been seeing things.

Walter nodded slyly at Yselle. Yselle winked back.

"All right," Terence said, "enough foolishness. Who wants to go first?"

Walter stepped forward. "I will."

Uxno, who had not seen him unplug the machine, gasped. "What courage! A true leader to the last! Walter Nutria, we salute you!"

"Solid," echoed Fip.

Walter shrugged. "Yeah, well . . ."

"Please stand there for a moment while I turn the machine on," Terence said. He flipped a switch. Nothing happened.

Terence flipped it off and on a few more times. Still nothing. Terence's lights flashed. "That's odd."

"Looks like it's broken," Walter said quickly, not giving Terence a chance to think. "What would Doctoral Candidate X want you to do now?"

"I don't know . . ."

"And he's not here," added Nurse Ratchet. "We can't ask him!"

Walter snapped his fingers. "I know! *We* could go ask him! We could fly out to the Terror Fleet, find out what he wants you to do with us, then come back and tell you. How does that sound?"

"You would do that for us?"

"Sure."

"Thank you all very much. You're very gracious to help like this." Terence's lights glowed warmly, and even Nurse Ratchet looked pleased. Slightly.

"All you have to do is show us to our ships," Walter said. "We really ought to hurry." Walter didn't know how long he would have until the robots figured out his trick, but he didn't want to press his luck by hanging around.

"Follow me, please."

"*These* are our ships?" wailed Uxno. He was right to wail.

"I think they took more than the Planetary Transponders," said Burkhardt.

They had come to the storage chamber that housed the *Gilded Excelsior* and the WSS *Ferlinghetti*, and found the two space vessels in the room or, more precisely, all over the room. Parts and sections from both ships were spread out on the floor. Important components had been removed, with the unwanted pieces tossed randomly in the corners. Cables hung through open access ports like cooked spaghetti. It was a mess.

"What did you do to them?" Fip was staggering around in little circles, trying to comprehend what he was seeing.

Terence wrung his enormous hands. "When you told me that these were your vessels, I was going to say something, but I didn't want to distress you."

"Yes, thank you. I feel *much* better," Voo said, kicking one of the *Gilded Excelsior*'s tires. It lay by itself on one side. The flying saucer was up on blocks.

Burkhardt had crawled under the hulk of the WSS *Ferlinghetti* and was examining the other side. "Hey! Where's the rest of it?"

"Yes, that's what I'm trying to say. This is very difficult after you've been so helpful and all," Terence said, "but the operatives took the useful parts from your vessels and put them in different ships of the Terror Fleet."

"Isn't there anything we can do?" Nurse Ratchet asked Terence hopefully.

"We could rebuild their vessels with our supply of spare parts, but that would take too long." Terence thought deeply. "Wait! We can send them off in the Supplementary Vehicles! Hurry! Come with me! If you're going to deliver a message to the Chief Executive Officer, there's not a moment to lose!"

If the regular ships of the Terror Fleet had been put together from random pieces of stuff, the two spacecraft in the Supplementary Vehicles Room seemed to have been made from the random pieces of stuff that nobody else wanted. Even on the ground, sitting perfectly still, they looked as if they might fall apart at any second.

Terence, however, insisted that they could fly. "They are just as space-worthy as any other ship in the Terror Fleet," he said.

Voo shook her head. "No way."

"These Terror Fleet Supplementary Vehicles were left behind as a backup, in case any of the regular Terror Fleet ships ran into mechanical problems before leaving for Earth. You can tell that by their names. They aren't official Terror Fleet ships, so they can't have terrifying names, but since they are backup vessels, they can have names that are almost terrifying, but not quite."

"The TFSV *Startling* and the TFSV *Mildly Upsetting*," Walter said, reading the designations spray-painted on the two spaceships.

"They are just as reliable as the regular ships, and probably even faster, since they don't have their cargo holds full of Space Mice and miscellaneous equipment for conquering the universe."

Terence's optimism was not shared by anyone. But there was really no choice, and time was running out. So, crossing their fingers (those who had fingers), Walter, Yselle, Burkhardt, and Snartmer climbed up a rickety ladder and into the *Startling*. Uxno, Fip, and Voo squeezed through the narrow hatchway on the *Mildly Upsetting*.

Terence pressed the Auto-Launch button on the wall, and the engines on the two ships began to warm up.

"Do you think they'll really find the Chief Executive Officer?" Nurse Ratchet asked.

"I believe so," replied Terence.

As the noise of the engines increased, the hatch door on the *Startling* suddenly flew open. Walter leaned out. "By the way," he shouted, "you may want to check the machine's power cord. It may be unplugged."

Terence waved at him. "That's an excellent suggestion! I'll try that!"

"If the machine comes back on, you'd better test it, just to make sure everything works. Try running those people in the jars back through it—that should let you know."

"Thank you again!"

Walter slammed the hatch door shut and grinned. If the robots went along with his suggestion, maybe Doctoral Candidate X would have an unpleasant surprise waiting for him when he returned to his fortress.

Terence and Nurse Ratchet watched the two junk ships rise out of sight.

"We'll have to check the cord right away," Nurse Ratchet said. "Wouldn't it be wonderful if we could fix the problem before the Chief Executive Officer even gives us directions?"

"It certainly would." Terence scanned the stars for any last glimpse of the two vessels. "You know, I think those were the most considerate prisoners we have ever had here."

32

The TFSV *Startling* was larger than the TFSV *Mildly Upsetting*, so Walter, Yselle, Snartmer, and Burkhardt had taken that one. The *Mildly Upsetting* had a lot less free space. It could hold Uxno, Voo, and Fip only if Fip stayed in the cargo hold and Uxno stood in the bathroom while Voo piloted the ship. Neither Fip nor Uxno was happy at all about this, but there was no other choice.

Aboard the *Startling*, they had a different problem. The bridge was large enough for everyone to be in it at once, but no one was small enough to operate the controls. Everything related to driving the ship, from the tiny viewscreen to the tiny cup holders on the tiny Naugahyde chair, was the right size for a Space Mouse from Galaxy Four. Unlike on the *Mildly Upsetting*, there was no dual set of controls that could be used by a Lirgonian or a high school freshman. Walter, Yselle, Snartmer, and Burkhardt were trapped on a spaceship that they couldn't steer.

Snartmer knelt in front of the tiny controls, trying to see the viewscreen, which was the size of a postage stamp. After a few minutes of this, he gave up. He got back to his feet slowly, his knees cracking with the effort. "It's hopeless. We'll never be able to work those controls. We can't even use the radio to call the other ship for help. We are really stuck, guys."

"We were able to work the Space Mice's backpacks, right?" Walter said. "Why can't we do the same thing here?"

"Those just had one dial and a button—we could work those with a chopstick. This time, it's the complete controls for an Intergalactic-Capable spacecraft. It's more complicated."

"Is it? It looks just like the Shrike Avenger video game. At least, I think so. If I had a magnifying glass I could tell for sure. In the game, all you have to do is—" Walter prodded the little steering wheel with the tip of his finger, and the *Startling* spun wildly.

"See! I told you! I told you!" Snartmer yelled, hanging on to a support beam while the ship rolled. "We're too big!"

"What about this?" Burkhardt pointed to a tan machine that the Space Mice had used to form part of the hull. "This is an Orion Industries Shrink-O-Tronic Device. Can we use this?"

The ship was still spinning, and Yselle was clinging to the ladder that led down to the cargo hold. Carefully, she leaned over to where Burkhardt was pointing. "How does it work?" she asked.

"I don't, like, know exactly. I bet you probably hit this button." As Burkhardt was indicating the right button, the ship lurched and his tentacle accidentally jabbed it. A beam of purple light shot out of the machine and past Burkhardt's head.

Yselle stared at the device. "What the heck was that?"

"You got me," Burkhardt said. "Hey, the ship's stopped."

They both turned toward the front of the bridge. Next to the pilot's chair stood Snartmer, smiling happily. In the tiny chair, working the tiny controls, was Walter. Walter was very, very tiny.

Once Walter had gotten the vessel back under control, he tried the Short-Range Space Radio. "Hello, do you read me? Hello, this is the TFSV *Startling* calling the TFSV *Mildly Upsetting*. Is there anybody there?"

"This is Voo. How's it going, Walter?"

"Fine now, I guess. We just managed to get the ship under control."

"Just now? It took you that long? What's wrong with you?"

"Thanks, Voo. Nothing's wrong with us. Well, something's wrong now, but I'll explain later. What next?"

Walter heard a faint voice over the radio saying something, but he couldn't make it out.

"What was that, Voo? I couldn't hear you."

"That was Uxno. There's no room on the bridge, so he's yelling orders from the bathroom. He says we should head straight to Earth. Are you ready?"

"Sure. How do we get there?"

"Just follow me. It's not far, only a couple of galaxies away. What time is it?"

Without thinking about it, Walter checked his watch. "A quarter to six. Why?"

"Good. The traffic should be pretty light. Let's go." The *Mildly Upsetting* switched into high gear and zipped away, with Walter and the *Startling* following it. Walter was lucky; the controls were just like the video game's and very easy to use. In fact, they were the actual controls from a Shrike Avenger game that had disappeared from a repair shop in Vancouver, British Columbia, nineteen months ago. The Space Mice had used the Shrink-O-Tronic to reduce them to the proper size.

Voo was right. It was a short trip. Before they knew it, they had entered Earth's solar system and sailed past Jupiter. Since Snartmer, Burkhardt, and Yselle couldn't see what was happening on the little screen, Walter had to describe everything as they went along.

"Okay, we're going through the asteroid belt now. Gee, Voo really drives fast. The speedometer says we're going at over 60 million Vultors per second, whatever that means. All right, I can see Mars now. We're getting closer. We're right next to Mars now. Wait a minute. Voo's brake lights are on. She's stopping. Why's she stopping? We're supposed to be going to Earth, what's she doing? Why's she . . . Oh."

The *Startling* had finally gotten far enough around Mars to see what had made Voo stop the *Mildly Upsetting*. It was the rest of the Terror Fleet. Hundreds of ships, all looking like things made from leftover model-kit parts, waited in orbit around the red planet.

"This must be their staging area," Snartmer said. "Doctoral

Candidate X didn't want to frighten the Earthlings with the entire fleet, so he had them wait here. Once he finds the plans for conquering the universe, he'll come back."

"How do you know all this?" Yselle asked.

"It's just common sense. I mean, if I was going to conquer the universe, that's how I'd take care of it."

"That's great," squeaked Walter from his chair, "but what do we do now?"

"I don't know," said Snartmer.

Then a new voice crackled over the radio: "Attention! Attention! Space Vehicles TFSV *Mildly Upsetting* and TFSV *Startling*! This is Space Mouse Alpha Platinum Alpha 0A0, commanding the Terror Fleet Flagship *Bonechilling*. What the heck are you doing?"

Knowing that the voice came from a creature that was only two inches tall didn't make it any less frightening. For a time, no one said anything. Eventually, Voo asked, "What do you mean?"

33

That wasn't what the Space Mouse Commander wanted to hear. "What do you mean 'what do I mean'? You know exactly what I mean! We didn't send a request for the Supplementary Vehicles, and yet here you are! I want to know why!"

"To be honest with you, that's a very good question," Voo said.

"Tell him you have an emergency message for Doctoral Candidate X," shouted Uxno from the bathroom.

Voo turned the microphone back on. "I remember now. There was a big problem back at the base. We have to deliver a message to The Boss. Is that okay?"

There was silence. Over on *Startling*, Walter could imagine the Space Mouse Commander trying to decide whether this was a trick or not.

Eventually the Commander said, "Well then, if this is such an important big deal, what's the Super-Secret Emergency Password?"

"Umm . . . The password . . ." Voo tapped her mittens nervously on the steering wheel. Uxno, who had previously been full of advice, had now decided to shut up. "The password is . . . 'pancakes'?"

"Hah! Wrong! There's no such thing as a Super-Secret Emergency Password! A real Space Mouse would have used the Normal Everyday Emergency Password! Impostors! Terror Fleet, attack!" On the viewscreen, Voo could see the hundreds of other spaceships turn slowly in the direction of the *Mildly Upsetting* and the *Startling*.

Uxno, who was unable to stay away from the action any longer, charged out of the bathroom. "Are we under attack?" he said. "What's going on?"

"Captain!" Voo shouted. "Get back in the bathroom! There's no room in here!"

"You need my experience!"

"But I can't steer! You're leaning on me! The gearshift is digging into my ribs!"

"Learn to live with it, Voo. You always were a crybaby. Even Mom thought so."

"She did not!"

The argument was stopped by the sound of Fip pounding on the ceiling of the cargo hold. "Hey! What's happening up there? I can hardly hear anything!"

"We're under attack!" Uxno shouted toward the floor.

"What? Who sat on a tack?"

While the Wotwot and Lirgonian captains shouted back and forth to each other, Voo set the radio's frequency to communicate exclusively with the *Startling*. "Walter Nutria, can you hear me?"

"Yes, Voo. What are we going to do?"

"You make a run for Earth and find Doctoral Candidate X. We'll try to hold off the Terror Fleet."

"Do you think one ship has a chance against the entire fleet?"

"Let's put it this way: I don't think two ships will have any better chance. And someone needs to stop that madman."

Aboard the *Startling*, Snartmer spoke into the tiny microphone. "Wow, Voo, that's really noble," he said.

"Very cool. And I mean that," agreed Burkhardt.

"Just shut up and go already!" said Voo.

Walter nodded. "Good luck, Voo," he said, and pushed the *Startling*'s throttle up to TRULY EXCESSIVELY MAXIMUM. The spaceship flashed around the far side of Mars and disappeared before the Terror Fleet had a chance to stop it.

34

The Terror Fleet didn't worry about Walter and the *Startling* for long. They still had one ship left to deal with, and they were going to make sure it didn't get away. The fleet rapidly spread out around the *Mildly Upsetting* in all directions, cutting off any possible escape.

"This is your last chance, whoever you are," announced the Space Mouse Commander. "Surrender now or we will blast you into little pieces. Consider this a warning shot!" Two bright pink beams of energy shot out from the largest Terror Fleet vessel and slammed into the side of the *Mildly Upsetting*.

The Command Room shook. Down below, Uxno and Voo could hear Fip bouncing around in the cargo hold.

"Wow! That was a Dual-Output Harmonic Plasma Director with acoustic rechanneling! It had pink beams, too. That means it's a Series II model," Uxno said. "Those are extremely rare."

"It's a shame it's pointed at us."

"It really is."

"Last warning, thieves!" The Commander's voice came back over the radio. "No one steals from the Space Mice and goes out for cappuccinos afterward! All Terror Fleet vessels, prepare to fire!"

Voo looked at Uxno. Uxno looked at Voo.

"What do we do now?" asked Voo.

"What do you want to do?" asked Uxno.

From under the floor panels, they heard Fip shout: "Have we tried running?"

Just as the Space Mouse Commander shouted "Fire!" Voo elbowed Uxno out of the way and stepped on the accelerator, turning the steering wheel hard to the right. Lasers and phasers and torpedoes and all kinds of destructive things rained down on the spot where the *Mildly Upsetting* had been a second and a half ago.

Voo slipped the *Mildly Upsetting* between two approaching Terror Fleet vessels, and the chase was on. The fleet chased them all the way around Mars, around its twin moons, Phobos and Deimos, and also around Ralphie, the mysterious third moon of Mars that Earth scientists have yet failed to discover. Since the Supplementary Vehicle was lighter and more nimble, it was able to stay out in front of its pursuers, but not by much. Eventually, the chase was going to have to end, one way or another. And when Voo happened to glance down at the fuel gauge, she realized that the chase was going to end pretty darn soon.

"Um, Uxno, take a look at this." Voo pointed to the gauge.

"What is it— Eek!" Uxno saw. There was less than an eighth of a tank left.

"What's going on?" Fip had managed to pry loose one of

the floor panels. Now he could talk to Uxno and Voo without yelling, and if he leaned back he could nearly see what was happening on the viewscreen.

"We're almost out of gas," Voo said.

"That's just peachy."

Laser beams from the Terror Fleet zapped through space, forcing the *Mildly Upsetting* to weave and spin to stay out of their way.

"They're going to be really annoyed when they catch up to us," Voo remarked.

Uxno tried to pace, but since there wasn't even enough room to turn around, it didn't work out. "If only we had some way to slow them down."

"But we don't have any weapons," said Voo. "I checked. Not even an Anti-Meteor Gun."

They heard rummaging noises from the cargo hold. "Hey, there's a complete torpedo-launching system down here!" Fip shouted.

Uxno clapped his mittens together. "Ha ha! Once again we triumph over evil! Nice job of checking, Voo."

"But there aren't any torpedoes," Fip added.

Uxno sighed. "Darn."

Down in the cargo hold, Fip heard Uxno calling him. "Aren't there any torpedoes at all? Not even a little one?" Then he heard the sound of another laser grazing the side of the ship. Desperate, Fip searched one more time.

He stopped at the back of the hold. Part of the ship's engine housing was made of old bicycles. Fip reached up with a tentacle and spun one of the wheels.

Back in the Command Room, Voo was wondering whether she could convince the Space Mice that this had all been a big mistake when she heard Fip yelling.

"Voo, how far away are the Space Mice?"

"Pretty close," she said.

"Good. Let them get a little closer. Not close enough to catch us, but as close as you can get. Play it by ear."

"*What?*"

"Just do it, okay? I think I know how we can slow them down."

Uxno shouted through the hole in the floor. "What's going on down there? Did you find some torpedoes?"

"I did better than that, you'll see. Now, slow down!"

Anxiously, Voo let her foot ease off the accelerator pedal. The massive Terror Fleet began to look even more terrifying as it closed in on them.

The *Mildly Upsetting* was getting into perfect laser range, and the Space Mice knew it. They kept firing, and Voo had a harder and harder time dodging the beams.

There was no viewscreen in the cargo hold, so Fip had no way of knowing when the time was right to try his plan. It might not work at all, but if they were going to do it, they might as well do it at the right time. Timing is everything to a Wotwot. "How close are they?" he shouted.

"Real close!"

"I guess that's close enough," Fip said and activated the torpedo launcher. In a flash, a spray of red shiny things shot out from the rear of the *Mildly Upsetting* and into the Terror Fleet. Immediately, the ships of the Space Mice started to slow down and their tight formation began to spread out.

Uxno and Voo watched in fascination until Fip yelled at them to keep driving.

"What did you put in the torpedo launcher?" Voo asked as the *Mildly Upsetting* sped away from the Terror Fleet.

"Bike reflectors," Fip said. "As soon as I saw them I thought it might work. Those ships are all piloted by Space Mice from Galaxy Four, right? And we already know what a Space Mouse from Galaxy Four likes to do better than anything else, right? Pick up junk! Especially sparkly, shiny kinds of junk." Fip pounded his tentacles on the ceiling of the cargo hold, extremely pleased with himself. "So what's sparklier and shinier than a bike reflector? Fifty bike reflectors! There's no way they could pass it up!"

"Excellent work!" Uxno said. "A brilliant piece of deduction and clear thought. Especially from you."

"I heard that!"

"One other thing," Voo interrupted. "How long do you think those reflectors will keep the Terror Fleet occupied?"

"Not too long," said Fip.

"No time for donuts, Voo!" Uxno clapped her hard on the back. "Head for Earth with all possible speed!"

"Would you mind getting back in the bathroom, please? I can hardly drive," said Voo.

35

While Uxno, Fip, and Voo were in the middle of their terrify-ing chase around Mars, the TFSV *Startling* was gliding into the upper atmosphere of Earth.

Yselle watched the continents spin by. "It's good to be home." After dealing with palm-tree aliens, Debbie Crom-well, talking mice, and everything else, the Earth seemed so normal. The next time kids at school called her weird, she was going to laugh in their faces. They had no idea what weird was.

"We've still got to find Doctoral Candidate X," the shrunken Walter squeaked from his tiny pilot's chair. "If he finds that book and learns how to take over the universe, he'll be unstoppable."

"Oh, no doubt," Snartmer said.

Burkhardt scanned the clouds, looking for any sign of an-other alien spaceship. "Where could he be? When people try to invade this planet, where do they usually go?"

"A lot of them seem to land in Washington, D.C.," Yselle said, thinking back to all the movies she'd seen.

"Don't forget Tokyo," Walter added. "Tokyo's big, too."

"Well, which one should we try first?"

"We don't have to," Snartmer said. "I think I've finally figured this thing out." He held up one of the dozens of blinking, whirring electronic devices that the Space Mice had put onboard the ship. "This is a Transit Particle Density Evaluator. It measures transit particles, which are left by spaceship engines. If I adjust this right, it should tell us exactly where Doctoral Candidate X's ship landed." Snartmer fiddled with the controls some more.

"Well?" Burkhardt said.

"I'm getting a reading, but I'm having a hard time believing it."

"What does it say?"

"It says that Doctoral Candidate X landed at East Weston." Snartmer shook the machine. "That can't be right. If he's looking for the rarest book in the world, why would he go to East Weston? No offense, Walter, Yselle, but East Weston isn't exactly the literature capital of the planet."

Walter and Yselle stared at each other. Together, they said, "Moth Lowell's!"

E. Patterson Mothra Upanishad Lowell IV, better known as Moth Lowell, was the owner and operator of Moth Lowell's Hard-to-Find. It was an antiques store like the *Queen Mary* was a boat. Moth Lowell's Hard-to-Find specialized in the rarest of the rare and the strangest of the strange. If you wanted to own the solid-gold boot-lifts that Napoleon wore on his Egyptian campaign, Moth had them in a drawer. Moth had for sale a stuffed two-headed rat that would whistle

"Stars and Stripes Forever" when you stepped on the air pump in its tail. Moth had two rare first-edition copies of *Spooky Things in New England*, by the reclusive horror-story author P. H. Kraftwerk, and he had a pretty good idea where to find an autographed Honus Wagner baseball card. In short, if you were looking for something, Moth Lowell either had it or knew where to get it.

Over the years, the Space Mice from Galaxy Four had tried sixteen separate times to steal choice bits of junk from Moth Lowell's inventory, but they had never succeeded. Each time they had been foiled by Vespasian, Moth's faithful Irish water spaniel and, if you believed Moth, the smartest dog in the world.

Both Walter and Yselle realized that if anyone, even an evil maniac from another galaxy, was looking for something rare and unusual, Moth Lowell's would be the obvious destination.

Walter steered the *Startling* toward East Weston. He tried to stay inside the cover of clouds as much as possible, since he was afraid that a passing 747 might see them and call the Air Force. Soon he could see the small skyline of his hometown rising up from the horizon.

Walter announced that they were almost at their destination. "Land at the East Weston Central Junkyard," Yselle said. "We can hide the ship there. If we just park it on the street, it's going to look funny."

Cruising low over the city and hoping that no one looked up, Walter reached the junkyard. He gently settled the ship down in a back corner and shut off the engines. He then spun around in his Space Mouse–size chair and faced the others. "I think we're ready to go," he said.

"Well, sort of." Yselle glanced in the direction of the two aliens.

"What do you mean?"

"The four of us can't just go strolling down the street, Walter. People will take one look at Snartmer and Burkhardt and run the other way. It'll cause a panic."

Snartmer held up a hand. "Not to worry. Burkhardt and I have been thinking about this, and we've got the problem all solved."

"You're going to stay in the ship?" Walter asked.

"No way," said Burkhardt. "We found some costumes in the back. We're going to disguise ourselves!"

"As what?" Yselle was skeptical.

"As normal human people! No one will even know we're from out of town."

"Why would the Space Mice put costumes onboard?" asked Yselle.

"Who knows why the Space Mice do anything? They're crazy little guys."

"Let's see the disguises," Walter said.

Burkhardt and Snartmer disappeared into the back. The Lirgonian was the first to reappear.

"What do you think?" asked Snartmer. He was wearing a gray trench coat. Aside from the red pajama hood and the red pajama feet, Snartmer looked almost normal. At least, he looked normal enough for East Weston.

"That should work," Yselle said.

Snartmer swirled the trench coat around, admiring it. "It's not bad, is it? But wait until you see this! Come on out, Burkhardt!"

Burkhardt the Wotwot emerged. In his everyday life, Burkhardt looked like a giant rutabaga with tentacles. Now, in disguise, Burkhardt looked like a giant rutabaga with tentacles wearing a propeller beanie.

Snartmer gestured toward Burkhardt like a showroom model displaying a new car. "Isn't that great?"

Walter and Yselle were silent for a few seconds. At length, Walter said, "You've got to be kidding me!"

"What?" Burkhardt sounded astonished.

"That's it? That hat?" Walter shook his head. "That's your disguise?"

"What's wrong with it?" Burkhardt twirled the propeller roguishly. "This is perfect!"

"But you look just the same!"

"Man, don't you remember anything about old Earth TV? You always see kids running around with these hats on. And no matter how freaky weird those kids look—and they all do—everybody just lets them barge right into their homes. It's a flawless disguise!"

"But—" Walter began.

"You know, I think Burkhardt's right," Yselle said. "Now that I look at him for a minute, I really do think he's got a point. I don't say to myself, 'There's a hideous alien in a stupid hat.' I just say, 'Look at that stupid hat.' I think it'll work."

"It'll have to," added Snartmer. "That's the only thing Burkhardt could fit into."

After staring at Burkhardt for a little longer, Walter said, "Well, maybe so. After all, we aren't going to be out on the street that long, and I'm sure Moth Lowell's not going to mind." He hopped out of the pilot's chair and onto the floor. He was about as tall as Yselle's shoe. "Someone get me un-shrunk, and let's go."

Snartmer examined the Shrink-O-Tronic Device that they had used to miniaturize Walter. There was a long pause, then he said, "I think we've got a problem."

36

"What do you mean it doesn't unshrink?" Walter was hopping mad. Since he was only a couple of inches tall, he looked like an enraged bug.

"I mean it's an Orion Industries Shrink-O-Tronic Device, not the combination Shrink-O-Tronic and Enlarge-O-Tronic that they also manufacture. That one's more expensive."

"So is he stuck like this forever?" Yselle asked.

"No, not at all. We just need to get our hands on an Enlarge-O-Tronic."

"Great," said Walter gloomily.

"Of course, if Voo were here, she could rewire this to unshrink instead of shrink. I could try it myself, but I'm not really good at mechanical things. I might end up shrinking you even more."

Walter shook his head. "No, thank you."

"So what do we do now?" Yselle said. "How are we going to take him with us?"

"No problem." Burkhardt had just returned from the back,

carrying a bundle of green cloth. "I found another costume. Snartmer, put this in front of the Shrink-O-Tronic," he said.

Josef K. Freud, the owner of Perfect Every Time Dry Cleaning, walked home for lunch each day down Maple Street. Today, he noticed an odd group of people coming down the street in the other direction, away from the East Weston Central Junkyard and toward Moth Lowell's Hard-to-Find. He didn't pay much attention to them; they were only a man in a trench coat, a kid in an odd hat, and a girl with a parrot on her shoulder. It's a good thing he didn't look closer, since he would have noticed that the man in the trench coat was also wearing red pajamas, the kid was actually an enormous vegetable-shaped space monster, and the parrot was, in reality, a very small high school freshman in a very small parrot costume. A shock like that would have ruined his appetite for the boiled cabbage and roast beef that was waiting for him at home. Fortunately, he didn't look twice, which saved his lunch and allowed Walter, Yselle, Snartmer, and Burkhardt to reach Moth Lowell's undetected.

Moth Lowell's Hard-to-Find was a large place. The building used to house an entire mini-mall, but as the other stores moved out, Moth Lowell bought up the extra space, and he still had barely enough room for his entire inventory.

The brass bell over the door rang as they came in. It woke up Moth's dog, Vespasian, who had been napping behind the counter. Sleepily, he stood up on his hind legs to inspect them, with his front paws resting on the countertop. Vespasian, who had struggled with the Space Mice and knew all about aliens, was not alarmed. After another curious sniff or two, he dropped back out of sight.

Aside from Vespasian, the store was empty. Moth Lowell was nowhere to be found. Propped up in front of the cash register was a sign that read: BACK SHORTLY—PLEASE FEEL FREE TO BROWSE. THE DOG WILL SEE TO YOUR NEEDS.

"Terrific!" Snartmer said. "This is just great. Now what do we do?"

"Be cool for a second. The book has got to be around here somewhere, right?" said Burkhardt. "So let's start looking." He opened a large cabinet by the door and discovered a carefully arranged display of shrunken heads.

"Well, that's enough of that," he said, shutting the cabinet carefully.

"Why is Moth not here? Moth is always here." Still balancing on Yselle's shoulder, Walter flapped his wings in irritation.

"Do you have any idea where he could have gone?" Yselle asked Walter.

From behind the counter, Vespasian barked softly.

"Pardon me?" said Snartmer.

There were a few seconds of snuffling sounds, then Vespasian trotted out with a sheet of pink paper held delicately in his teeth. He dropped it at Yselle's feet and sat down.

Yselle read the paper. "It's an invoice. '45-rpm records, one crate, assorted modern masters, suitable for jukebox use. To be delivered today.' " Yselle glanced at the fake parrot on her shoulder. " 'To Nutria's Billiards.' "

Horton Nutria's pool hall was only a few blocks away,

and easy to find. No other building in town had NINE-BALL, EIGHT-BALL, SEVEN-BALL, THREE-BALL—TOURNAMENTS WEEKLY! and IF ALL TABLES ARE FULL, YOU PLAY FOR FREE—GUARANTEED! painted on the windows in two-foot letters.

Inside, a haze of cigar smoke made it hard to tell just how far back the rows of well-used pool tables stretched. Only a few of the tables were occupied. The pool players, mostly men in loud plaid sport coats, studied their games with complete concentration. No one even looked up when Yselle, Walter, Snartmer, and Burkhardt arrived. In one corner, a jukebox glowed with soft green-and-yellow light while it played "The Hula Hula Boys."

Walter noticed that Snartmer's eyes had gotten huge. He was trembling a little and gazing around the pool hall as if it was the most incredible thing he had ever seen.

"You hear about places like this," Snartmer said in a hushed voice, "but you never really believe it until you see for yourself. Unreal."

"There he is!" Yselle said, pointing. Over by the cashier's cage, Moth Lowell was talking to Horton Nutria while Horton signed a receipt. Yselle waved. "Moth!"

Moth Lowell was tall, with an extremely long neck. In fact, he looked a lot like an ostrich with glasses and a droopy mustache. "Hello there!" he said, folding the signed receipt and putting it in his pocket. "How are you, Yselle? Is this a new pet?" he asked, nodding toward Walter.

"Awk! Polly wanna cracker!" squawked Walter, trying his best to impersonate a parrot.

"Be quiet!" Yselle hissed.

"How you doin', Yselle?" Horton Nutria said, joining them. "It's been a while since you've been in here. Hey, have you seen my nephew Walter?"

Yselle shook her head while Walter, shrunken and disguised in a parrot costume, tried to look invisible.

"Well, if you do, tell him that he's gotta return that pool cue he borrowed. Paul the Flatfish is breathing down my neck about using that cue in the Tournament of Champions, and I don't want any trouble."

"Awk!" said Walter the parrot. The cue was in the back of his closet, where his mother couldn't find it. For the past month he had been meaning to sneak it out of the house and return it.

Yselle said she would tell Walter as soon as she got the chance. "And this is Snartmer and Burkhardt," she said, introducing the aliens. "They're just visiting." Yselle couldn't tell if Moth Lowell and Horton Nutria were truly fooled by the disguises, or if they were just being polite. "I don't mean to interrupt anything, but is there any way you could come back to your store with us, Moth? We're trying to find something special and really need your help."

"Why, certainly," Moth said. "I think we're all done here. If you'll excuse us, Horton."

"Come back any time," said Horton Nutria.

As they left the pool hall, Snartmer hesitated for a moment to have one last look around. He sighed. "Voo'll never believe it," he said to himself.

Back at Moth Lowell's Hard-to-Find, the store was still empty, and Vespasian was asleep again. "Now then, what can I do for you?" Moth asked, taking out his handkerchief and polishing a bust of Samuel Pepys.

"Awk! Book! Awk! Awk!" said Walter the parrot.

"We're looking for a book," Yselle explained. "We've been talking about it so much, the parrot must have memorized the word.

"Shut up," she whispered to the parrot on her shoulder.

"This is what parrots do," the parrot whispered back.

"It's very important that we find a copy of this book," said Snartmer. "We need it for . . . for . . ." Snartmer didn't want to say, "We need it for saving the universe," because that might give their disguises away, but he couldn't think of anything else.

Burkhardt jumped in. "It's for somebody's birthday. He has his heart set on this book."

"What's the title?"

"*Roger Rocket and the Pirates from Ganymede,*" all four of them, including the parrot, said together.

Moth tugged at his mustache, thinking. "*Pirates from Ganymede,* hmm . . . That's the rare one from the Roger Rocket, Space Hero series, isn't it?"

They all agreed that, yes, that was the book.

"That's odd. You're the second person to ask me about that today."

They all turned pale. "Did you give it to him?" Yselle asked, her voice trembling.

"Did I give him the book? Did I give him the book? Do you

know what? I can't remember. Vespasian!" Moth called. The Irish water spaniel trotted obediently out from behind the counter and sat down at Moth Lowell's feet. "Vespasian, do you remember that other fellow who came in here and asked about the Roger Rocket book?"

Vespasian whined.

"What happened? Did we sell it to him?"

Vespasian whined.

"Oh, that's right!" Moth tapped his forehead. "We didn't have that book in stock. I offered to sell him a copy of *Linda Carlton, Air Pilot,* the upside-down misprinted version, but he wanted *Roger Rocket.* He was very insistent about it."

"What happened next?" Yselle said.

"Where did he go?" Burkhardt said.

"What did we say, Vespasian?"

Vespasian whined.

"Yes, we told him to try looking in Evanston-Sturville. Evanston-Sturville is simply teeming with quality rare-book stores."

"Oh, great. Awk!" said Walter the parrot. Evanston-Sturville was thirty miles away, which meant that Doctoral Candidate X still had a head start on finding the book.

Moth noticed the crestfallen expressions on their faces. "What's wrong?"

"We were kind of hoping to find that book as soon as we could," Yselle said.

"Our friend's, um, birthday is tomorrow," lied Burkhardt.

Moth tugged his mustache again. "Well, I have been meaning to drive up to Evanston-Sturville to pick up some sixteenth-century maps I ordered. I could give you a ride if you like, and show you the most likely places to look, if you're interested."

"That would be great," Yselle said.

"Awk! Thank you! Awk!"

"Amazing!" Moth Lowell tried to look closely at Walter the parrot, who crawled up Yselle's collar and hid behind her head. "That is an astoundingly intelligent bird."

Yselle rolled her eyes. "Sometimes."

37

Moth Lowell left Vespasian in charge of the store while the rest of them piled into Moth's old Bentley and headed out. The ride was uneventful, except that Snartmer and Burkhardt kept getting into fights over who was taking up more of the backseat.

Moth drove them through the streets of Evanston-Sturville, stopping finally at a small downtown storefront. On the front window, McTavish's Rare, Used, and Rarely Used Books was written in fancy gold letters.

"This is it," Moth said. "McTavish specializes in rare books that are also actually fun to read. I suspect that he'll have a copy of your Roger Rocket book."

The four of them climbed out, thanking Moth for the ride. Moth offered to pick them up in an hour or so, but Yselle said they'd take the bus. Tracking down Doctoral Candidate X might take all afternoon. Moth waved and drove away.

On Yselle's shoulder, Walter tore the parrot mask off his head and threw it down. "That's enough!" he said. "I can't breathe in there! Anyway, if no one notices that Burkhardt's not a human being, no one's going to notice that I don't have a parrot's head."

Snartmer pointed impatiently in the direction of the bookstore. "Come on! We may be running out of time."

The inside of McTavish's contained nothing but books. Books on shelves, books on counters, books in boxes, books piled up on the floor. Except for the narrowest area for the customers to move through, every available cubic inch of space was taken up by books.

At the moment, there was only one customer in the store. He was short, thin as a rail, and wore a trench coat exactly like the kind Snartmer had taken from the *Startling*'s costume locker. They immediately noticed how tiny his head was, and how far his thin whiskers stuck out, and how his hair was an unusual shade of electric blue.

"I think that's a . . ." Snartmer whispered.

"You're right," Walter said. "I think you're right."

The mysterious figure glided to the back of the store, where George McTavish sat reading *The Proceedings of the International Society for the Promotion of Antique Books and Antique Booksellers.*

"Excuse me," said the mysterious figure in a high-pitched voice. "I have been searching for a copy of the exceedingly rare 1953 book *Roger Rocket and the Pirates from Ganymede.* Several of the other bookstore owners told me you might have one. Is that by any chance correct?"

McTavish sat up and put his paper away. "It certainly is." He stood on a stepladder to reach the top shelf behind his counter and took down a small hardback book in a plastic bag. "This is it," he said, holding it up. The brightly colored cover showed a boy in a space suit running across the surface of the moon, while a distant spaceship fired energy beams at him. "As far as I know, this is the only copy in North America."

Excited squeaking noises came from somewhere inside the mysterious figure's trench coat. "I want to buy it," the mysterious figure said.

McTavish checked the price tag. "It's pretty expensive."

"I don't care." The figure handed him a credit card.

"I've never heard of the First Bank of Galaxy Four," McTavish said, examining the card.

"It's new," the figure replied, swaying a little.

McTavish filled out the credit card form, tore off the receipt, and handed it to the figure, along with the card and the book. "There you go," he said. "I hope you enjoy it."

Over the sound of squeaky laughter coming from inside the trench coat, the figure said, "Oh, we will," and turned to leave.

The figure passed by Burkhardt, Snartmer, Yselle, and Walter on its way to the door. Its beady little eyes met Burkhardt's beady larger eyes. Then it looked from Burkhardt to Snartmer to Yselle, as if it was trying to remember their faces.

"Barry!" Yselle said, finally recognizing him. It was the Space Mouse they had captured and released on Ice Planet B.

"Run!" Barry squeaked. The figure threw open the door and launched itself into the street.

Before George McTavish even had a chance to say "May I

help you?" to the newcomers, they were all gone again, chasing the Space Mouse–headed figure down the block.

"Be careful! Slow down!" Walter shouted at Yselle. He was clinging to one of her jacket's metal snaps for dear life.

"Hang on! Almost there!" Yselle was nearly close enough to tackle the mysterious figure, who was half running, half stumbling, a few steps ahead. Snartmer and Burkhardt, neither of whom was built to move very fast, trailed behind.

The figure turned a corner, and Yselle was able to grab the tail of its trench coat. She pulled, hoping to trip the figure up, but instead it wriggled free and kept running, leaving Yselle holding the coat. Without its disguise, the figure looked pretty much like what they'd suspected. A Space Mouse on stilts was the figure's legs. Sitting on the shoulders of the first Space Mouse, another one held the sticks that were the figure's arms. On the ends of the arm-sticks were two remote-control hands, one of which held the book. Sitting on the shoulders of the second Space Mouse was Barry, who had played the figure's head by simply poking his own head out of the trench coat's collar.

As ungainly as all this looked, it could run very fast. Yselle and the others were still chasing it when it reached Harangue Park. Harangue Park was named after Evanston-Sturville's most famous citizen, the legendary football coach Gunther Harangue. At the other end of the park there was a statue of Gunther Harangue that scowled down upon the swing sets and monkey bars. Currently, though, the view of the statue was blocked by the huge spaceship that sat in the middle of the park.

Yselle, Burkhardt, and Snartmer stopped suddenly. Walter, who was not expecting this, nearly flew off Yselle's shoulder again. He was lucky that he didn't—the parrot costume, while realistic, was not aerodynamic at all and Walter would have fallen like a stone.

The spaceship was dark crimson, made up mostly of angles and sharp points and sinister-looking decorative flourishes. Steam curled from its powerful engines. The Space Mouse stick figure ran around behind the ship, but its pursuers were not paying attention.

The four of them had been distracted by a small spacecraft, one that looked like it was made out of unwanted random junk, gliding down from the sky.

38

As they watched, the TFSV *Mildly Upsetting* settled un-steadily onto the ground between them and the crimson spaceship. Nothing happened for a few seconds, then the door opened and the stairs rolled out. Uxno and Fip appeared in the doorway, fighting to be the first to climb down. The struggle was so intense that they ended up falling out together, hitting the grass with a thump that made Snart-mer and Burkhardt wince. Voo quietly climbed down after them.

The others rushed over to greet them.

"Captain! You made it!" Snartmer said, shaking Uxno's mitten warmly.

"What happened? Are you all right?" asked Burkhardt.

Fip stared at Walter. "Forget about us. What happened to him?"

"We had to use the Shrink-O-Tronic on him to make him small enough to work the controls on our ship," Yselle said.

"Voo, Snartmer told me you can undo this," Walter said. "Can you?"

Voo squinted at Walter. "Hmmm . . . I think the *Mildly Upsetting* uses an Enlarging Beam Generator as part of its engine. Let me go check." Voo disappeared back up the ship's ladder.

"You know," Fip said, "I can't help but notice that *our* general is still normal size."

"So what?" Uxno said defensively. "Our general may be very tiny, but his heart is big and his brain is mighty." Uxno noticed Walter's headless parrot costume for the first time. "Well, probably, at least."

"It's you!" said a voice they all recognized. Doctoral Candidate X appeared from behind the crimson spaceship. He was followed by hundreds of electric-blue Space Mice and held *Roger Rocket and the Pirates from Ganymede* in his hands. "How did you escape my robots?"

"It's a long story," Uxno began.

"Forget it! I don't care! How did you escape my Terror Fleet?"

"They're busy," said Voo.

"They're chasing shiny bike reflectors around Mars," said Fip.

"Arrgh!" Doctoral Candidate X tore off his space helmet and threw it to the ground. "Stupid Space Mice! Stupid Space Mice and their stupid fixation on stupid shiny things! Why did I ever put you in charge of anything?"

"Boss, I'm sure there's a reason . . ." said Barry the Space Mouse.

"Be quiet!" In his fury, Doctoral Candidate X kicked at Barry the Space Mouse and connected, sending Barry flying over the nearby buildings in a graceful arc.

"Soooooorryyyyy, Boooooosss . . ." squeaked Barry as he disappeared from sight.

"The jig is up, evil guy," said Fip.

"Yeah!" agreed Burkhardt.

"You and your Space Mice are no match for us, not on this planet, not now that we're all together again!" Snartmer said.

"Oh, the jig is up, is it? Is it?" Doctoral Candidate X clasped his hands together in pretend terror. "We're not a match for you? Me and my Space Mice? What about me, my Space Mice, and my *giant robot?*"

Doctoral Candidate X took a remote control from his lab coat pocket and pressed a button. The top of the sinister crimson spaceship opened up, and a giant robot stepped out to join him and the Space Mice. The robot was even larger than Terence, and this one looked like it was in a bad mood.

"Robot smash!" it grunted.

"Hey, wait a minute," Yselle said. "You told us you were only coming to Earth to find that book. Why did you need to bring a giant robot?"

Doctoral Candidate X chuckled. "My dear girl, I was merely thinking ahead. You should know that every serious plan for conquering the universe requires a giant robot at some point. By bringing it with me, I was saving time."

"Found it!" This was Voo, calling out from the door of the *Mildly Upsetting*. In her mittens she held a complicated-looking ray projector. She aimed it at Yselle's shoulder. "Hold still."

"No! Wait! Not now!" someone yelled, but it was too late. Voo activated the Enlarging Beam Generator. It sent out a yellow ray that hit Walter, but Walter must have moved a little, or Voo didn't aim exactly right. Either way, part of the beam missed Walter and hit the giant robot.

In a flash, Walter and his headless parrot costume were back to normal size. That was the good news. The bad news was that Doctoral Candidate X's giant robot was now twice as giant.

"Robot *really* smash!" it grunted.

"Thank you, Voo, thank you very much," Uxno said, staring at the enormous robot.

Voo leaped to the ground and joined the others. "I didn't see them," she pleaded. "I didn't know they were there!"

"Silence!" Doctoral Candidate X threw up his arms in a grand mad-scientist gesture. "No more talking from any of you! Now I talk!" He tore the plastic wrapping from his copy of *Roger Rocket and the Pirates from Ganymede.* "Now I learn the foolproof plan for conquering the universe, and there's nothing you can do about it!"

They watched, frozen in terror, as Doctoral Candidate X opened the book and flipped through the pages. "Aha! Page 121!" He began to read out loud:

> "But professor," asked Roger anxiously, "can the Ganymede
> Pirates really take over the universe?"
> Professor Astro's careworn, intelligent features were grave.

"I'm afraid they can, Roger. Unless you and the Star Patrol can stop them."

"But how can they do it? How can anyone take over the entire universe?"

"It's very simple, actually. Follow me." Professor Astro strode purposefully to the space chalkboard and picked up a piece of atomic chalk. "You see, conquering the universe requires only Five Easy Steps. Step One . . ."

39

"Arrgh! No!"

Everyone stared at Doctoral Candidate X.

"It's not here! It's not here!"

"That doesn't sound like much of a first step," Uxno whispered to Walter.

"The pages are missing! Someone tore the pages out!" Enraged, he turned to the assembled Space Mice. "Someone must pay for this! Bring me the bookseller! Now!"

He didn't have to tell the Space Mice twice. They disappeared in the blink of an eye.

"What do we do now?" Yselle whispered to Fip.

"Should we grab him?" Fip whispered to Voo.

"He's all by himself," Voo whispered to Walter.

"Except for that robot," Walter whispered back.

"Robot can hear you from over here," grunted the enormous robot.

Doctoral Candidate X threw the book down. "This is not fair! This is simply not fair! But I will not be stopped! I will conquer the universe! I will!"

The Space Mice, with the memory of what happened to Barry still fresh in their little mouse minds, wasted no time in hurrying to McTavish's Rare, Used, and Rarely Used Books, grabbing George McTavish, and hurrying back. It happened so quickly that George McTavish didn't have time to drop his cup of coffee before it was all over and he found himself staring into the angry spectacles and bushy eyebrows of Doctoral Candidate X.

Doctoral Candidate X thrust the book in his face. "What is this?"

McTavish blinked. "It's the Roger Rocket book I just sold to that skinny guy with the blue hair. Why?"

Doctoral Candidate X picked up the wrapper and shook it. "This says 'near mint'! How can you say this book is in near-mint condition when it has a bunch of pages ripped out! The important pages, too! How fair is that?"

"For an evil maniac, he's awfully touchy," remarked Snartmer, quietly.

McTavish examined the wrapper. "Okay, I see. Look here." He pointed to the label. "It doesn't say 'near mint,' it says 'near mints.'"

"What?"

"That's my own personal cataloguing system," McTavish explained. "It helps me out when I'm trying to tidy up the store. 'Near mints' means that this book goes on the same shelf where I keep my box of peppermints. See how that works?"

Doctoral Candidate X made a strangled noise in the back of his throat.

McTavish, unwisely, went on. "You thought this book was in near-mint condition? Oh, no. I'd guess its condition is probably fair to critical, especially with those missing pages. It's so expensive because it's so rare. If it was in near-mint condition, too, I could buy another house with it."

"Why didn't you say pages were missing when you sold it?" Doctoral Candidate X shouted.

"I didn't know. I've never read it. Personally, I read *Tom Satellite of the Outer-Space Rangers.*"

"You see, it's hopeless," Uxno shouted. "This plan is doomed to failure. Give up your evil schemes, finish your education."

"It will make your parents happy," added Snartmer.

"Never!" Doctoral Candidate X said. "Never! I'll prove to you that I can be an intergalactic overlord! I'll prove it to everyone!"

"What are you going to do? You don't have the right pages!" said Walter, who was starting to feel brave again now that he was back to the right size.

"Oh, yeah? Well, no more Mr. Nice Madman, kid. I'll find another copy of the book! I'll send my Space Mice to invade every used bookstore on this puny planet! I'll use my enormous robot to tear up every library!"

Doctoral Candidate X spoke into his remote control: "Attention, Terror Fleet! Stop chasing those stupid bike reflectors and listen to me! The plans have changed! Every ship is to land on Planet Earth immediately! Find me that book! Take no prisoners!"

He turned his attention back to the others. "And now I'll deal with you! Robot, smash!"

"Smash!" repeated the enormous robot, and it took a step forward.

40

Up until that moment, George McTavish thought the robot was just another piece of oversize sculpture that someone had set up in the park, a modernist companion to the statue of Gunther Harangue. When he realized it was alive, and angry as well, that was too much. He dropped his coffee cup and ran for the safety of McTavish's Rare, Used, and Rarely Used Books as fast as he could go.

Yselle watched McTavish retreat. "Do you think we should run, too?"

"The robot would probably follow us," Walter said.

"Smash!" said the enormous robot, enjoying its job.

"If we can't run, I say we go down fighting!" Fip said. He waved his tentacles in a threatening manner.

"Remember, getting squashed in the line of duty is the ultimate test of dignity. Let's all be mature about this," said Uxno.

"Smash!" said the enormous robot, getting closer.

"I am really getting tired of this," said Voo.

"I wonder if the robot has an off switch," said Burkhardt.

"It's probably too high to reach," said Snartmer.

Doctoral Candidate X laughed. "Squirm, worms! Even as you meet your doom, the advance scouts of my Terror Fleet arrive! Look to the sky!"

High above, two spaceships were descending rapidly upon Evanston-Sturville. As they got closer, it was possible to tell that one of them looked like a stainless-steel flying saucer and the other one like a long, narrow rocket ship with big tail fins.

"Are those . . ." Walter said.

"Those aren't . . ." Doctoral Candidate X said.

As everyone, even the enormous robot, watched, the *Gilded Excelsior* and the WSS *Ferlinghetti* landed in Harangue Park.

The doors on the two space vessels opened, revealing Nurse Ratchet and Terence.

"Sir! Chief Executive Officer! Sir!" Nurse Ratchet waved anxiously. "We have a message for you!"

"We wanted to let you know that the Unpleasant Machine was working properly again. We thought it might be important, so we repaired these vessels and—"

The rest of what Terence said was drowned out by the hordes of people who were muscling their way out of the *Gilded Excelsior* and the WSS *Ferlinghetti*. Pushing and shoving, they gathered in a large, angry group around Doctoral Candidate X.

"You idiot!" Doctoral Candidate X screamed above the noise of the crowd. "What have you done?"

"Once the Unpleasant Machine was plugged back in, we had to test it, sir," Terence said. "Lacking any new prisoners,

Nurse Ratchet and I ran these people through the reverse process."

"When we were convinced the machine worked properly, we tried to put them back in their jars, but they refused to go! They insisted on seeing you first," Nurse Ratchet said.

"And you let them?" Doctoral Candidate X was now almost completely engulfed by the crowd, some of whom were holding up papers and blue examination books.

"They were very determined, sir," Terence said. "They positively refused to wait."

During the confusion, Walter, Yselle, the Lirgonians, and the Wotwots ran toward the robots and their spaceships.

"Who are all those guys?" Burkhardt asked Terence.

"If I remember correctly, they were his academic advisers, his parents, several former lady friends, and a number of his students with ungraded classwork. They all appeared to have various grievances with him, but they did not share that specific information with me."

Doctoral Candidate X's head appeared above the crowd. "Robot! Don't just stand there! Get them!" he shouted before disappearing again.

The enormous robot swiveled around to face Walter, Yselle, and company. "Smash again!"

"Montague!" Terence cried. "What in heaven's name has happened to you?"

"Robot get big!" grunted the giant robot, who was, apparently, known as Montague.

"What have we discussed about your grammar?"

"Sorry," said Montague. "*I got* big. I was accidentally hit with an enlargement ray."

"That's better."

"Should I smash them now?"

Terence's lights blinked indignantly. "I think not. Smashing people is hardly civilized behavior."

While this discussion was going on, the crowd had picked up Doctoral Candidate X and were carrying him toward the crimson spaceship. Over the angry shouts of "Where's my grade?" "Where's your annotated bibliography?" and "You're such a disappointment!" Doctoral Candidate X could still be heard yelling: "This is not over! You haven't heard the last of me! I'll be back! Believe it! Believe it! I *will* rule the universe!"

The crowd carried him aboard the crimson spaceship and closed the door behind them. Soon, the engines roared to life and the ship took off.

Between the *Gilded Excelsior* and the WSS *Ferlinghetti*, the others watched in silence until the ship had disappeared from view. Then Terence sighed and said, "You probably wouldn't want to come back and be our prisoners again, would you?"

"No," said Walter.

41

"Did you know that was going to happen?" Yselle asked. "Did you know those people would track down Doctoral Candidate X if they got out of their jars?"

Walter shrugged. "I had an idea, but I wasn't sure. I figured the more people running around mad at him, the better."

They were watching the two Wotwots and the three Lirgonians check over their ships before taking off. Neither group had enough crew members to pilot their ship properly, but with a little luck they would be able to get them safely back to Planet Wotwot and Planet Lirg, respectively.

"You know," said Terence, who was standing behind them, "I'm still a bit displeased with you for tricking us as you did."

"Oh, let it go," said Nurse Ratchet. "As much as I hate to admit it, maybe we'll be better off without the Chief Executive Officer."

"Perhaps you're right. He could be rather imperious at times. Still, what will we do now that he's disappeared? We have that entire facility in Galaxy Four, and nothing to use it for."

Voo tapped Terence on the arm. "I know someone who

could help you out," she said. "Her name's Spherical Mattress Stoyanovich. I'll find you her intergalactic telephone number. She could give you a hand."

"Or at least a thumb," remarked Walter.

"When I last checked, the Space Mouse operatives were still pursuing those bicycle reflectors around Mars, in direct contradiction of the Chief Executive Officer's last command," Terence said. "Eventually, though, they're going to get tired of it and realize that they no longer have jobs. Do you think this Stoyanovich person could possibly find some employment for them?"

Voo snorted. "Thousands of tiny junk freaks? Sure, Stoyanovich could use them for something."

Montague the robot, now no longer enormous, closed an access panel on the TFSV *Mildly Upsetting*. "Your modified de-enlarger ray seems to work, Voo. I believe this little craft is ready to fly."

"It's out of fuel, though," Voo said.

"No problem—I siphoned some gas from that Buick over there. It's enough to get Terence, Nurse Ratchet, and me home."

Fip and Burkhardt joined them. "We're ready."

"So are we," said Snartmer, coming down the *Gilded Excelsior*'s stairs with Uxno.

Terence looked around at the three space vehicles crowded into Harangue Park. "I suppose we should be going. It wouldn't do to make trouble for Walter and Yselle by alerting the general public."

"Don't worry about it. Nobody ever pays any attention to what happens in Evanston-Sturville," Walter said.

Yselle frowned at Uxno and Fip. "I hate to bring this up, but aren't you two supposed to be at war with each other? What's going to happen when you get home?"

"That . . . Yes . . ." Uxno kicked a pebble with the toe of his pajamas, and Fip turned green, which is the Wotwot way of blushing.

"We decided to call it a draw," Fip said.

"I mean, if the two greatest space generals in the entire cosmos can't get a victory for either one of us, maybe we weren't meant to be fighting in the first place."

"But we aren't—" Walter started to protest for one last time but decided to forget about it. "Good idea," he said instead.

There were a few more goodbyes, and everyone began climbing aboard the spaceships.

The *Mildly Upsetting*, the *Gilded Excelsior*, and the WSS *Ferlinghetti* took off. Only a few feet off the ground, the WSS *Ferlinghetti* lurched unsteadily and bumped the *Gilded Excelsior*. The flying saucer wobbled, and before it could right itself it neatly decapitated the statue of Gunther Harangue. The *Gilded Excelsior* hovered for a second, as if deciding whether it should land and apologize, then rose quickly into the sky.

Yselle, Walter, and the severed head of Gunther Harangue watched the ships get smaller and smaller overhead.

42

They both knew it would be a pretty smart thing not to stay too long in Harangue Park. Even in Evanston-Sturville, someone was bound to show up eventually and ask questions.

They took an intercity bus back to East Weston. Walter kept looking up at the sky, to see if he could catch a glimpse of the *Gilded Excelsior* or a stray spaceship from the Terror Fleet. He kept expecting the bus to transform itself into a flying robot or the driver to announce that he was actually from Pluto. Over the past couple of days he had gotten used to everything being more weird than he had ever imagined, and now that things were back to normal, it seemed even stranger.

Once they arrived in East Weston, Walter and Yselle stood on the corner of Mordant Boulevard and Philomena Avenue. "I guess I'll see you at school tomorrow," Yselle said.

"I guess so." It was getting cold. Walter shivered.

"What do you think your parents are going to say?"

Walter shook his head. "I don't know. What about yours?"

"They usually don't mind whatever I do. Of course, I've

never been gone this long before. I guess I'll find out. See you later, Walter."

"Bye."

They went off in opposite directions, each heading for home.

When Walter reached his house, he had barely gotten the door open before he learned how his parents had reacted to his disappearance.

They had flipped out.

"Walter!" his mother shrieked. "Where on earth have you been?"

"What's the big idea, Walter? Do you know how worried your mother has been?" shouted his father.

"When we read that horrible note you left, we thought it was just a prank, but when it got later and later and you didn't come home, we were frantic!"

"Your mother was frantic," his father said. "I was angry. And I still am. If you think you can pull a stunt like this and still rent all those videotapes, you have got another think coming, mister!"

"We called that store where you get all those tapes, and they said they hadn't seen you. Your uncle Horton said he didn't know where you were, either. He also told me that you borrowed his best pool cue last month and needed to return it."

"Is that true? Have you been down at that pool hall again?" asked his father.

Walter nodded. He wasn't really paying attention. He was staring at a much-abused cardboard box sitting on the hall table. The package was covered with odd stickers and stamps, and it was held together with masking tape. It was addressed to him.

"I even called the parents of that horrible Meridian girl, but there was no answer. You weren't off with her, were you?"

"No, Mom," Walter said automatically. The postmark on the box was shaped like a flying saucer.

"We were just about to call the police, but your uncle Horton convinced us that you would be back soon enough."

His father laughed. "Horton just hates the thought of getting anywhere near the police, that bum!"

"Arthur! Be quiet! Walter, are you listening to us?"

"Yes, Mom." Walter tore the box open, ripping through a label that read Time-Space Courier Corporation.

"Walter!"

Inside was a pink plastic object shaped like an ugly water pistol. It had a handle and a trigger and a flared barrel, and a small gold sticker on the side. Walter turned it upside down so he could read the print on the sticker. It said: Orion Industries Mind Control Device.

"Walter, give me that thing this instant. We're not through talking to you!"

Walter looked at his parents, then back down at the Orion Industries Mind Control Device. He didn't say anything. He couldn't possibly be in any *more* trouble, he thought.

"Walter!"

Walter pointed the device at them and pulled the trigger.

A field of pulsating pink light surrounded his parents, and they froze in place. Walter held the trigger down.

"Can you hear me?"

Mr. and Mrs. Nutria nodded stiffly.

"Raise your right hand."

"We hear and obey." Both of them raised their hands.

Walter knew what he was supposed to do. "Okay," he said, "you will forget that I was ever gone. As far as you know, I came home from school at the normal time, just like always."

"We hear and obey."

Walter glanced inside the open box and saw a note, half buried by the bright yellow wood shavings that the ray gun had been packed in:

> *Walter Nutria, we apologize profusely that we were unable to return you to your planet in a time machine, so Voo, Snartmer, and I chipped in and sent you this token of our appreciation by Better-Than-Instant Delivery. We hope it arrives in time to take care of any difficulties you may experience.*
>
> *With the greatest possible sincerity,*
>
> *Uxno*

It looked like the Lirgonians had gotten him out of trouble, but Walter didn't turn the Mind Control Device off. How often did an opportunity like this come along?

"From now on, you will let me rent R-rated movies."

"We hear and obey."

"Even *Slavegirls from Beyond Infinity?*"

"We hear and obey."

This was too good to be true.

"And you won't freak out if I ask Yselle Meridian to the Tulip Extravaganza?"

"We hear and obey." It took them longer to answer this time. Walter knew his mother must have been fighting the device's control.

"Hmmm . . . And I think you should—" Walter kept the trigger of the Mind Control Device firmly pressed, but the pink field around his parents started to flicker.

"Ow!" Walter dropped the device. It had shocked him, and now he could see black curls of smoke rising from it as it lay on the hall floor.

"Well, hello, champ," his father said, rubbing his eyes. "How was your day?"

"Walter, did you wipe your feet?" His mother looked around. "You did just come in, didn't you?"

"That's odd. I thought Walter had come home from school at the normal time, just like always."

"So did I, Arthur. But why else would we be here in the hall? No matter, I suppose. Let's go see what's in the fridge for supper. Walter, wipe your feet."

As soon as his parents were gone, Walter ran to the phone and dialed Yselle's number. "Hey, it's me," he said when she answered. "How did it go? Are your parents mad?"

"That's kind of a funny story."

"The Lirgonians sent me some sort of mind-control thing, and I was able to make my parents forget about everything. You can try it on your folks if you want. I think I may have shorted it out, though."

"It's okay. My parents are fine with it," Yselle said. "I don't even think they knew I was gone."

"For real?"

"Yeah. When I got home I found my mom and dad inside these two giant plastic pods, like the depressurization tubes in *This Island Earth*. I think they're suspended-animation capsules or something. When I got my parents out, they thought it was still Tuesday. I guess I'll have to explain it to them somehow."

"That's great," Walter said. "Listen, Yselle."

"Yes?"

Since he had already brainwashed his parents about the Tulip Extravaganza dance, he might as well go ahead and ask Yselle. "I, um . . ."

"What is it?"

"I'll . . ." This wasn't getting him anywhere, and he was starting to get embarrassed. "I'll see you at school tomorrow, okay?"

"Sure. Bye, Walter."

Walter hung up. He wondered if the Mind Control Device had any power left in it.

43

The next morning, Walter realized that he had been less worried about how his parents would react than he was about going back to school. He wasn't afraid of getting in trouble for being gone—he had already written a fake excuse note in his mother's handwriting. Instead, he was afraid that school was going to seem even more pointless than before. After all, once you've traveled to distant planets and risked your life in interstellar spacecraft battles with beings from another galaxy, there's not much about first-period history that's going to hold your interest.

The day started out pretty much like normal. No one noticed that he had been gone. In Mrs. Baucomb's history class, the usual half-asleep feeling descended on him, smothering him like an old scratchy blanket. He stopped listening. He stopped paying attention at all and started wondering how he could pass the time after he cut school at lunch.

This lasted all through English, and into economics. Then he noticed the empty seat where Debbie Cromwell usually sat. Debbie Cromwell was still away "visiting colleges." While the teacher droned on about profit and loss, Walter started thinking about Debbie Cromwell, who was really Hhh, assistant fashion engineer from Planet Pentathlon. Walter was surprised to find himself getting angry. He was angry that he had to come to East Weston Northside High every day and sit in his chair and be bored to death. He was angry at the teachers, the ones like Mrs. Baucomb who didn't care at all, and the ones like Mr. Murphy who just didn't make any sense and then told you it was *your* fault for not figuring out their code. And Walter was angry at himself, for having sat there and taken it all this time without complaining.

But now things were going to be different. He had seen too many of the exciting things outside to sit there and become a zombie again. He may have to go to school, but now he was going to make sure he enjoyed it.

The next period was study hall. After roll call, where he answered "present" to both his name and Timmy Arbogast's, Walter started work on his biology report for Mr. Murphy.

"And that is the vital role that coniferous trees play in the world's ecosystems."

"Very nice, Prudence," Mr. Murphy said, making a mark in his grade book. Prudence Tesla nodded at Walter on the way back to her desk. Walter nodded in return. He was ready to go.

Mr. Murphy checked his list. "And the next report we have today is by Walter Nutria."

Walter walked to the front of the class and put his notes on Mr. Murphy's podium. He cleared his throat. "As you all know, my report is on deciduous trees. Deciduous trees are those trees that shed their leaves on a regular basis.

"I'm sure you also know that they grow in temperate climates, and they are home to all sorts of animals. These include snails, turtles, owls, woodpeckers, rabbits, bears, deer, chipmunks, and, of course"—he nodded to Mr. Murphy— "skinks.

"What you may not know is that the word *deciduous* was first used in 1883 by Professor Roland Flang. He was the first person to photograph a sensitive striped spitting skink and live, but he is probably most famous for discovering the electric blue skinks of Greater Macronesia."

The rest of the class sat up straighter and started to listen with interest. By this point in the school year they had all become skink experts and were in danger of running out of fresh skink facts to add to their own reports. Any new information about these uninteresting little lizards was sure to show up in everyone else's future presentations.

"It began in 1906," Walter said, "when Professor Flang was on an expedition to the Metaluna Islands. One evening, while he was walking back to his base camp, he was ambushed and kidnapped. Warriors from the island of Lirg had heard about the professor and thought he would make a perfect general to lead them into battle against a rival island. By the time the Lirgonians had explained their plan to him, they were out on the open ocean, and Professor Flang had no choice but to agree."

Walter could tell the report was going over well. Even Mr. Murphy had taken his eyes off the skink tanks and was paying attention. Set in the South Pacific, instead of outer space, Walter's story sounded amazingly believable. It was a shame Yselle didn't share this class with him. She would have loved the performance.

"When they stopped on Stoyanovich Island to pick up supplies, Professor Flang heard about the electric blue skinks for the first time. At that time, people knew next to nothing about these creatures. The electric blue skinks often stole small objects, just like the pack rats of North America, but what they did with those things was a mystery. Some people said the skinks took them to Australia, and some said New Guinea. No one knew."

Walter went on to tell about how Professor Flang met the fierce Wotwot people, and how both groups became marooned on Ice Island B after the electric blue skinks raided their equipment.

Walter noticed a few strange looks in the audience. "Ice Island B is a weird name for an island close to the equator," he admitted, "but it's really true. I looked it up."

As the class listened, Walter described how Professor Flang and the Lirgonians, along with the Wotwots and the Wotwot commander, tracked down the skinks and foiled the plans of the madman who had been behind it all.

"By preying on the natural gullibility of all skink species, they were able to defeat Tribal Shaman X and restore peace to the islands," concluded Walter. "And in doing so, Professor Flang learned more about the electric blue skink than anyone who had ever lived. His book, *Small, Blue, and Scaly: A Guide to the Skink Populations of the Pacific*, is still the best book on the subject, even after all these years. I would have brought a copy with me, but our library keeps it in the reference-only section. Thank you."

It was a thrilling report, full of action and interesting details. And it also had nothing to do with real skinks. Roland Flang was the name of a billiard hustler Walter's uncle Horton Nutria knew.

Walter wanted to see if anyone would mention that his entire report was fiction, or if anyone would even notice. He wanted to find out who was crazier: Mr. Murphy for creating his unspoken requirement that every project had to do with skinks, or the students for following it. He knew that he probably wouldn't find out by making up fake reports, but it was a lot more interesting than just sitting there and playing along.

At the end of his presentation, the students clapped, and even Mr. Murphy said, "Nice job, Walter." Walter sat back down at his desk and looked around. His heart was pounding. He had gotten away with it. This was going to be fun.

44

That afternoon, instead of sneaking out the front door of
the school, Walter checked to make sure that no one was
around and let himself out the back.

Behind East Weston Northside High was the teachers'
parking lot. Behind that was the football stadium, home of
the Fighting Hyraxes. Walter headed in that direction.

There were a lot of kids back behind the stadium, talking in
little groups or standing around trying to look sophisticated.
Walter found Yselle sitting on a wire milk crate next to one of
the stadium's support beams. She was playing chess on a tiny
portable board. Her opponent had a patchy, thin beard and
wore a Northside baseball letter jacket.

Yselle moved her bishop and noticed Walter standing
nearby. "What are you doing here?" she asked. "I thought you
always took off in the afternoons."

Walter shrugged. "Yeah. I guess I just felt like doing something different today."

"Well, I'm glad to see you." She stood up and looked at the

chessboard. "Mate in five moves, Marty. Can we call it a game?"

Marty studied the board for a second, then snorted and knocked his king over. He lit a cigarette and started gathering up the pieces. "Next time, Meridian. Next time," he said, but he didn't sound too confident.

"Come on, I'll show you around," Yselle said to Walter. "You know, I was kind of hoping that you'd show up here."

"You were?"

"Sure."

Walter didn't know what to say after that. He wanted to tell Yselle that he was glad to hear this, but he didn't want to sound stupid. One of his uncle Horton Nutria's favorite pieces of advice was "When in doubt, keep your big yap shut." So they just kept walking. They passed a group of kids sitting on the ground, listening to an old man in a coat and tie play a banjo.

"That's Mr. Oswic, one of the physics teachers," Yselle said. "He's out here a lot. He makes sure we don't fall off the top of the bleachers or whatever, so the rest of the teachers kind of leave us alone."

"He doesn't look like he's keeping an eye on anything," Walter said, watching him concentrate on the banjo.

"He isn't. In fact, we had to drive Annika Vergmuller to the emergency room a couple of weeks ago. Those seats are higher than they look."

Walter watched the kids milling around, the football field, and the school beyond that. "Doesn't it seem so weird that we're here again? I mean, where were we yesterday? Ice Planet B? The Space Mouse planet?"

"Yeah. Today I'm supposed to be in study hall, and you're skipping gym. Just like always."

"Pretty much," Walter said. "But not exactly." He told her about his adventure in Mr. Murphy's Skink World that morning, and his plans to enjoy school from now on.

Yselle laughed out loud, causing two girls in black sweaters and pale makeup to turn around and stare. "Walter, that's priceless! What are you going to do about Mrs. Baucomb?"

"I don't know yet. I'll think of something, though."

From across the football field they heard the bell ring.

"That's chemistry," Yselle said. "I gotta go."

As she started to disappear, Walter called, "Hey, do you mind if I meet you here again tomorrow?"

Walter thought she said, "I wish you would," but he couldn't be sure. It didn't matter. He still felt so pleased with himself that he almost ran all the way down to The Lonesome Skillet. Almost.

Walter began to spend more and more of his time behind the stadium. He slowly learned to play chess, though it was obvious that he was irredeemably bad at it. Even Mr. Oswic could beat him regularly. He saved a little dignity by being the best by far at movie trivia. He noticed that talking to Yselle and the other kids about movies and ways to distress his teachers was a lot more fun than waiting for the video stores to open.

One afternoon he and Yselle were sitting by themselves on

top of the grandstand. "You know, I've been thinking," Walter said slowly.

"Southside Video has a bunch of new films in their foreign section," Yselle said, not listening. "Do you want to watch some this weekend?"

Walter tried again. "Well, I've been thinking about that."

"About what?"

"Ever since, you know," he pointed to the sky, "we got back, things have been really kind of nice."

"Walter, what's wrong?"

"Nothing! I mean, everything's fine."

"Then what's going on?"

"It's just . . ."

"What?"

"Do you want to go to the Tulip Extravaganza with me this Friday?" Walter said in a rush.

Yselle did not start laughing. And she did not fall off the back of the grandstand in shock. Walter was relieved.

Instead, she said, "Really?"

"Yeah. I thought it would be fun."

"Sure."

Walter had seen a lot of movies with romantic subplots, so he knew enough to act nonchalant, as if there had never been any doubt in his mind.

"Great," he said, pretending not to be relieved. "Pick you up around eight?"

45

Walter was nervous. For the third time he checked his hair in the rearview mirror.

"Hey! Do you mind? I'm trying to drive up here!" This was Jimmy "Twelve-Toes" Fortinbras. Jimmy Twelve-Toes was the owner of a limousine company, and he spent a lot of time at Horton Nutria's pool hall. He owed Horton a favor, and he had agreed to chauffeur Walter and Yselle to and from the dance. It was clear that Jimmy Twelve-Toes was not wild about this.

The limousine pulled to a stop outside Yselle's house. "Okay, kid, you're up," Jimmy Twelve-Toes said.

Walter checked again to make sure his tie was straight. He got out of the limousine and knocked on the Meridians' front door. He waited there, tapping his foot and watching Jimmy Twelve-Toes watch him for what seemed like an hour until Yselle opened the door.

"Hi, Walter," she said.

Yselle was wearing a black dress, like the one Barbara Rush

had worn at the end of *It Came from Outer Space*, when she tried to lure Richard Carlson into the aliens' cave. Walter, who had never seen Yselle in anything other than jeans and her old police jacket, didn't know what to say. The truth is, Walter thought she was gorgeous.

"Um, hi," he said at last.

"Hi."

Walter remembered he was carrying something. "These are for you," he said, holding out a small corsage. He had traded his authentic shooting script of *Reptilicus*, complete with handwritten director's notes in Danish, to Moth Lowell for a silver corsage holder that Moth swore had once belonged to Anne Boleyn, the second wife of Henry VIII.

Yselle pinned on the corsage. "Thank you, Walter. You look very nice, by the way."

"Thanks. Are you ready to go?"

"Let me get my coat."

At the dance, Walter and Yselle met up with some of the other kids from behind the football field. They all sat together for a while, listening to the band and talking about where to eat after the dance. Walter recommended The Lonesome Skillet. Then he laughed.

"What is it?" Yselle asked.

"You know, I just realized—I haven't been to The Lonesome Skillet for weeks. Or even to my uncle's pool hall."

"Does that mean you're turning into a human being, Walter?"

"I guess so. Sort of. Maybe. Wanna dance?"

"This is a lot of fun," Walter said as they danced to Zip Holliwell and the Star-Tones' rendition of "Since I Don't Have You." On the other side of the dance floor, Debbie Cromwell was dancing with Spencer Zyblut, who was captain of the football team and, probably, an actual human being. Over Yselle's shoulder, Walter saw Mrs. Baucomb standing by the wall with the rest of the chaperones. She was staring at him. Walter smiled broadly and waved.

Walter had become Mrs. Baucomb's least favorite pupil. A couple of times a week, while she solemnly read from the textbook, Walter would raise his hand. This was something that had never happened to her in the past eleven years. First, she tried ignoring him, but then Walter would wave his hand urgently and make "Ooo! Ooo!" noises. When she finally called on him, Walter would ask things like, "Was the Teapot Dome scandal about real teapots? What kind of tea did they use?" Or "Did the G in Warren G. Harding stand for 'Grover'? How about 'Gargantua'?" They were harmless questions, but they disturbed the peace of the classroom, which drove Mrs. Baucomb nuts.

Now, she would glance nervously at Walter every few minutes and count the days until she could hand him off to Mr. Tremayne in world history.

"Anyway," Walter said to Yselle, "I just read in the paper that there's a new art-movie house opening up in Evanston-Sturville. Would you want to go with me sometime?"

"I'd like that, Walter."

Walter decided to press his luck. "And maybe we could get some dinner or something, too?"

"That sounds good. We ought to run by McTavish's and see how he's doing," Yselle added. "I think he nearly had a heart attack last time when we—" She stopped dancing.

"What's wrong?"

"Nothing, I mean, I just remembered something. Sit down and I'll be right back."

Walter took a seat at an empty table. In a minute, Yselle returned. She was carrying her coat. "There's somebody I want you to meet," she said.

Walter glanced around. He thought he had already met all of Yselle's friends, even Mr. Oswic, who was by the punch table, looking lost.

"Check this out." She reached into her coat pocket and pulled out a tiny ball of electric blue fur.

Walter stared at it, amazed. "Barry!"

"In person!" squeaked the Space Mouse.

"I was getting ready for the dance tonight, and I heard something tapping on my window. I checked, and there was Barry!" she said. "He'd lost his teleportation backpack, and a cat was chasing him."

"I only knew a couple of people on this planet, and I thought maybe we could make a deal, you know?" Barry said.

"A deal for what?" asked Walter.

Yselle smiled. "Listen to this."

"I mean, you guys seem like reasonable people. She gave me cheese." He nodded at Yselle. Then he turned to Walter.

"And you, well, the girl digs you, so I guess you're tolerable."

"You dig me?" Walter asked Yselle.

"Walter, pay attention!"

"Now here's the deal: I'm stuck on this planet, right?" Barry said. "You guys have a spaceship hidden somewhere around here, right? But you're too big to fly it, right? So how about the three of us get together, and I'll fly us to Space Station Stoyanovich? I can get a ride home from there, and I'll have my buddies pick you up some big-size controls for your ship. Space Mouse's honor. No fooling." He squeaked hopefully. "How about it?"

"What ship?" Walter said.

The Space Mouse rolled his eyes and Yselle explained. "The *Startling*, remember? The one with the tiny little controls? The one we landed in the East Weston Central Junkyard? Well, it's still there!"

"Oh! Seriously?"

"Seriously!" Barry said. "Come on, what do you think?"

"What do I think?" Walter looked at Yselle. Her eyes were bright. She seemed excited. "What do you think?"

"It's a short trip," she said. "Why not?"

Walter was thrilled. "Okay, then. Let's go!"

"Too cool!" squeaked Barry the Space Mouse. "Grab your coats. And keep watching the skies!"